Alexandra Hopewell, LABOR COACH

Dori Hillestad Butler

Albert Whitman & Company
Morton Grove, Illinois

Library of Congress Cataloging-in-Publication Data

Butler, Dori Hillestad.
Alexandra Hopewell, labor coach / by Dori Hillestad Butler.
p. cm.
Summary: Eleven-year-old Alex Hopewell wants to be her expectant
mother's labor coach, but first she must convince her family, friends, and
teacher that she can handle the responsibility.
ISBN 0-8075-0242-1 (hardcover)
[1. Responsibility—Fiction. 2. Pregnancy—Fiction.
3. Childbirth—Fiction.
4. Schools—Fiction. 5. Learning disabilities—Fiction.] I. Title.
PZ7.B9759Al 2005 [Fic]—dc22 2004018344

Cover illustration by Wayne Alfano.
The design is by Carol Gildar.

For more information about Albert Whitman & Company,
visit our web site at www.albertwhitman.com.

For Ben.

Alexandra Hopewell,
LABOR COACH

1

"Alexandra Hopewell! I hope that wasn't your family life project that just went flying across the room."

Alex jumped when she heard the sharp tone of her teacher's voice.

It *used* to be her and Reece Burmeister's family life project. Now it was just a gooey, yellow mess dripping down Reece's Minnesota Vikings shirt.

"I-I didn't mean to," Alex whimpered.

"Didn't mean to!" Reece yelled as egg guts dribbled from his shirt to the floor. "Look at me! I'm covered in egg." He turned to Mrs. Ryder. "Alex threw an egg at me!"

Alex gasped. "I didn't throw Eggbert! I-I tossed him. Reece told me to."

"I did not!"

"You did, too! Didn't he, Miranda?"

Miranda sat behind Reece. She had to have seen and heard the whole thing. But she just sat there like a lady in church, her mouth zipped shut. Nobody else spoke up in Alex's defense, either.

Mrs. Ryder rose slowly from her chair.

Alex tried one more time to explain. "Reece kept going 'Psst! Psst!' He held out his hands like he wanted Eggbert. So... I sort of tossed him over. But then Reece put his hands down. He didn't even try to catch Eggbert. He wanted Eggbert to break because he wanted to get me in trouble."

"That's enough!" Mrs. Ryder banged her fist on her desk.

Alex swallowed hard. She was in trouble now. So what else was new?

"Honestly, Alexandra. I don't know where your mind is." Mrs. Ryder came around her desk. Melanie, Justin and Kaila all shrank back in their seats as Mrs. Ryder moved toward Alex. Alex's friend, Ben, glanced at her with sympathy.

"We don't throw eggs across the room." Mrs. Ryder declared, hands on her hips. Her whole face matched the blood red lipstick she wore every day. "You're in fifth grade, Alexandra. I shouldn't have to tell you that!"

Alex twirled her braid around her finger and did what she always did when Mrs. Ryder yelled at her. She counted the wrinkles on Mrs. Ryder's forehead. *One wrinkle, two wrinkle . . .*

"Just how many eggs have you broken now, Alexandra? Three? Four?" *Five wrinkles, six wrinkles . . .* "How many?" Mrs. Ryder demanded.

Seven wrinkles, eight wrinkles . . .

"Nine," Alex said out loud.

"NINE broken eggs?" Mrs. Ryder screeched.

"Huh?" Alex blinked. "No, I mean three," she said quickly. Three broken eggs. Eggbert the first, who accidentally rolled off her desk. Eggbert the second, who accidentally got squashed when Reece set him on Alex's chair. And now Eggbert the third. And this was only the second day of the family life unit.

Mrs. Ryder shook her head sadly. "I don't think you're taking this project very seriously, Alexandra."

"I am, too," Alex said. Then she clamped her hand over her mouth. She was arguing again. Mrs. Ryder had called Alex's parents last week to complain that Alex was *argumentative*. While she was at it, Mrs. Ryder also complained that Alex was careless, loud and unfocused.

Alex had promised to do better. To *be* better. But if being better meant pretending you were married to Reece Burmeister and the two of you had an egg for a baby—well, Mrs. Ryder had to expect a few mistakes.

"Reece, why don't you go down to the bathroom and clean yourself up," Mrs. Ryder said. "And Alexandra?" She had that I-just-don't-know-what-to-do-with-you look on her face. "Go get some paper towels and clean up this mess."

No one in the class said a word. But everyone was staring at her. Alex could feel their eyes boring holes into her back as she slunk to the back of the room and

3

yanked out a wad of paper towels from the dispenser above the sink.

Using her thumb and first finger, Alex carefully picked up the broken eggshells. There was one piece that had part of Eggbert's smile and another piece that had part of his hair (hair that Alex had pulled from her very own hairbrush). Poor little Eggbert, Alex thought as she stacked the pieces off to the side.

Miranda slid her blue shoes out of the way. "You're making more of a mess," she whispered as Alex smeared the sticky goo around in a circle.

"So?" Alex whispered back. "Who asked you?"

When Reece returned, there was a huge wet spot across the front of his shirt. "I think you should change your name from Alex Hope*well* to Alex Hope*less,*" he told Alex as he sat down in front of Miranda.

"Shut up," Alex said.

Mrs. Ryder went to her supply closet. "I've got one more egg here." She held it up so everyone could see the B that she had stamped on the bottom. The B meant it was a boy.

"Since you've had so many problems with this project, Alexandra, I think I'm going to let Reece take this one by himself." Mrs. Ryder lumbered toward Reece.

"All right!" Reece smirked at Alex.

"What?" Alex rose up onto her knees. How could Mrs. Ryder let Reece take care of an egg by himself? Reece hadn't even taken Eggbert home last night like he was supposed to. When Alex found out, he told her he'd smash her face at recess if she told Mrs. Ryder.

But now Reece leaped out of his chair and pretended he was a good and caring "dad." He carefully cupped his hands around the egg Mrs. Ryder brought him. "Oh, my poor baby," he said. "He comes from a broken home."

Stafford and Drew snickered. Even Mrs. Ryder smiled a little.

"If Reece gets that egg by himself, what am I supposed to do for my family living project?" Alex asked in a small voice. She knew Mrs. Ryder wouldn't let her get away with doing nothing for this project.

"You can write a report on some aspect of child development." Mrs. Ryder tucked her silver hair behind her ear. "I'd like to see a topic sentence and a list of three sources on my desk tomorrow morning." Mrs. Ryder loved topic sentences and lists of sources.

"B-but that's not fair," Alex dropped her wad of wet paper towels. "Nobody else has to write a report."

"And nobody else has broken three eggs," Mrs. Ryder pointed out. "You've completely missed the point of this assignment, Alexandra."

"No, I haven't. The point is to show we know how to take care of a baby. And I know all about that because my mom's having a baby in a few weeks and—"

"If she knows what's good for her, she'll keep you far away from it," Reece muttered.

Alex stomped her foot. She'd had enough of Reece Burmeister. This was all his fault. "For your information, my mom isn't just going to let me take care of it, she's going to let me see it be born," she heard herself say.

Miranda's bottom jaw dropped open.

"She is," Alex insisted. "I'm going to help out in the delivery room and I might even cut the umbilical cord. Now that's real family life."

Everyone stared at her in stunned silence.

Then Mrs. Ryder pinched her lips together and said, "Yes, well, why don't you finish cleaning up the floor while the rest of us go to music." Her shoes clicked against the floor as she marched to the door. "Rows one, two, three, four and five. Line up. Let's go."

Without a word, the whole class got up and followed Mrs. Ryder out the door. Ben lagged a little behind everyone else. He and Alex had lived next door to each other practically their whole lives. He knew

Alex better than she knew herself. Which was probably why he raised an eyebrow at her.

Alex looked away. Okay. So what she said wasn't exactly true. It still felt good to say it. Besides, it was *possible* she could talk her mom into letting her be there when the baby was born. Anything was possible.

2

"There's no way your mom is going to let you be there when she has that baby," Ben told Alex on their way home from school.

"She might." Alex gazed at the boy egg that Ben carried on a bed of paper confetti inside an old soup can. The soup can was covered with blue fabric and trimmed with lace. "Olivia Greene got to be there when her mom had a baby. And she's only eight."

Ben shifted his can to his other hand. "Yeah, but the Greenes are weird."

That was true. The Greenes lived across the street from Alex, but they weren't like any other family in the neighborhood. For one thing, Mr. and Mrs. Greene homeschooled Olivia because they thought the public schools were bad. They had a computer, but no TV or radio. They ate weird food like seaweed and tofu. And they didn't take any medicine, not even Tylenol, because they thought it was bad for you.

But they let Olivia be there when her baby sister was born. They had a midwife instead of a doctor and Olivia's mom had the baby at home. Olivia said that seeing a baby be born was the most amazing thing that ever happened to her.

"This isn't just something I blurted out," Alex told Ben. "I've thought about this for a long time. I really do want to see the baby be born." Alex bent down and picked a daisy from the side of the road. "I heard my mom talking on the phone to my Aunt Cindy last night. She's afraid my dad won't be home when she has the baby."

Alex's dad was a pilot. When he flew, he was usually gone for several days at a time.

"My mom told my aunt that she was going to ask your mom to be her back-up labor coach."

Ben pushed his glasses up. "What's a labor coach?"

Alex raised an eyebrow at Ben. "You don't know?" Ben was the smartest kid she knew. He was so smart he skipped kindergarten. But he sure didn't know much about having babies.

"A labor coach is someone who rubs the lady's back when she's having a baby and gets her a glass of water and reminds her to breathe." Alex had seen it all on TV.

"Oh." Ben did not look impressed.

"I was thinking maybe I could be my mom's back-up labor coach instead of your mom," Alex said as they crossed a street.

Ben stared at Alex. "You?"

"Yes, me! Why not?"

"You're a kid," Ben said. "And you're not even twelve years old. Don't you have to be twelve to visit people in the hospital?"

"I wouldn't be visiting, I'd be helping," Alex said as one by one she began plucking petals from the daisy. *Mom WILL let me be there when the baby's born, Mom WON'T let me be there when the baby's born,* Alex thought to herself with each petal she plucked. Oh, she hoped Mom would let her!

"Yeah, but still," Ben said. "You're..." his voice trailed off.

"I'm what?" Alex looked at him.

Ben scratched his ear. "Well, no offense, Alex, but you're not exactly the sort of person people want around in an emergency. Remember last year when we had that tornado warning during school?"

Alex remembered. When the sirens sounded, everyone went out in the hall. People were supposed to sit down on the floor and put their heads on their knees. But Alex had sort of run around yelling, "We're all going to die! We're all going to die!" until the counselor, Ms. Westley, came and calmed her down.

"This is totally different." Alex said as she continued to pull petals from the daisy. "For one thing, having a baby is not an emergency."

"You have to go to a hospital to do it."

"You don't have to. Olivia's mom didn't."

"Yeah, but most people do. Your mom will."

Alex was almost all the way around the whole flower. She could just count the rest of the petals to find out whether Mom would let her be there when the baby was born or not, but it seemed like that would be cheating.

"Okay." Ben snatched the daisy out of her hand. "Even if your mom says you can go to the hospital, and even if the people at the hospital say you can be there, I still have one more question."

"What?"

Ben wrinkled his nose. "Why would you *want* to?"

Alex grabbed the daisy back. "Because!"

"Because why?"

How could she explain it? "Because having a baby is a big deal. Because I never thought my parents would have another kid. Because Olivia got to do it. I don't know. I just do."

Mom WILL let me be there when the baby is born! That was where Alex was when she plucked the last petal from the flower. She unzipped the front pocket of her backpack and slipped the daisy stem inside for good luck.

"Okay," Ben said in a weird voice. Alex could tell he didn't get it at all.

* * *

Alex's dad liked meat, potatoes and vegetables with every meal. So when he was away, Mom and Alex ate things like pizza, spaghetti or tacos. Tonight they were having take-out Chinese.

While Mom emptied the bag, Alex couldn't help but stare at her mom's huge round stomach. It looked like a dinosaur egg was stuck under her shirt.

"Do you want an egg roll?" Mom asked.

Alex shuddered as she shook her head. She didn't want anything to do with eggs.

"Sweet and sour chicken?"

Alex shook her head again. She wasn't crazy about things that *laid* eggs, either. "I'll just have rice." She knelt on her chair and dumped some steamed rice onto her plate.

Mom helped herself to an egg roll, chicken and steamed rice. Then she sat down next to Alex. "How was your day, honey?"

Alex stirred her rice around. "Eggbert the third got broken."

"Oh no!" Mom looked sorry, but not really surprised. She knew Alex.

Alex tried to explain how it was mostly Reece's fault, but Mom didn't pay any attention to that part. "You *threw* an egg across the room?"

"I didn't throw him very hard. And Reece was supposed to catch him." Alex dropped her eyes to her lap. "Now Mrs. Ryder *really* hates me."

"Oh, Alex. She doesn't hate you."

"Yes, she does," Alex insisted. "She won't let me carry an egg around anymore. She says I have to write a report instead."

Alex hated writing reports.

"Well, I know you didn't mean to break those eggs, but you have to admit, three broken eggs in two days is a lot."

Alex shrugged.

Mom patted Alex's knee. "I'll help you with your report," she promised. Then, tilting her head toward Alex's plate, she said, "You'd better eat."

Alex popped a forkful of rice into her mouth. Then she stirred the rest of her rice around some more. "I already have an idea for what I could do my report on," she said as she shifted nervously in her seat. She glanced at her mom from the corner of her eye.

"Mm?" Mom raised her head, but her mouth was too full to talk.

Alex lowered her eyes. "Of course, Mrs. Ryder

would have to wait about six weeks for the report, but that would be okay."

Mom swallowed. "What's your idea?"

"I could . . . go-to-the-hospital-and-watch-a-baby-be-born," Alex said in a rush.

"I don't know, honey," Mom said as she dabbed the corners of her mouth with a napkin. "Most women wouldn't be comfortable—" She stopped. Her eyes widened to the size of golf balls. "You mean me? You want to watch me have the baby!"

"It would be for school," Alex explained quickly.

Mom shook her head. "I don't think so."

"Why not?"

"Alex, having a baby is a very personal thing. I couldn't go through labor and delivery with an audience."

"I'm not an audience. I'm your daughter. I promise I won't be in the way. I won't say a word. Not unless you want me to. And I could help. I heard you tell Aunt Cindy you need a back-up labor coach, in case Dad is away the day you go into labor. You don't have to ask Kate to be your back-up labor coach. I could do it. I could hold your hand and get you water and tell you when to breathe." Alex had to stop there so *she* could breathe.

Mom sighed. "I don't know, honey."

"Please, Mom! I really want to see the baby be born."

Mom peered deeper into Alex's eyes. "This isn't just about your report, is it? You really *do* want to be there when the baby's born."

Alex grabbed her braid and twirled it around her fingers. "Uh huh." She nodded. She really did want to be there.

Mom sighed again. "Well, I can't make a decision like this on the spur of the moment. Let me talk to your dad. I'll need some time to think about this."

"Okay," Alex said. But she couldn't wait around for Dad to get back so he and Mom could talk about it. Mrs. Ryder wanted to see a topic sentence and list of sources on her desk *tomorrow*. If Alex didn't have a topic sentence and list of sources, there would be even more trouble.

3

A cold, steady rain fell the next morning. It was too wet to walk to school, so Ben's mom picked Alex up. As soon as the Casey's white mini van pulled into the driveway, Alex flew out the door and down the front walk.

"Hi, Kate," Alex said to Ben's mom.

"Hi, Alex." Kate smiled. "Don't you want a jacket?"

"Huh?" Alex looked down at her bare arms. She didn't have any goosebumps, so it couldn't be all that cold. "No, I'm okay."

She climbed into the van and plopped down on the bench next to Ben.

"Watch it!" Ben grabbed his soup can and held it away from Alex. "You almost sat on Ernie."

"Sorry," Alex said, shifting over.

"Miranda will kill me if you break our baby." Ben patted the egg's head.

Alex rolled her eyes. "Your baby is fine." She buckled her seat belt as Kate backed down the driveway. "Will you read my topic sentence and list of sources for my report?" Ben was good at topic

sentences and lists of sources. He was good at everything school-related.

"Let me finish my pick 'ems for this week. Then I
will, okay?"

Alex hadn't noticed the notebook in Ben's lap. Ben
didn't play football, but he was probably more into the
sport than kids who did play. He knew all the profes-
sional teams and who was playing whom each week.
His main hobby was predicting which teams were
going to win each week.

Ben tapped his pencil against his chin like he was
thinking really hard. Alex peered over his shoulder to
see which teams he was trying to decide between.

Baltimore vs. Dallas.

"Pick Baltimore," Alex said.

"Why?"

"Because I've been there. They've got a cool aquar-
ium. I've never been to Dallas. I don't know what they
have."

Ben pushed his glasses up on his nose. "You can't
pick a team based on whether you've been to their
city or not. You have to look at the teams themselves,
the stadiums they're playing at, whether any of their
players are hurt, that kind of stuff."

Alex thought that was too much trouble. She liked
watching football with her dad, but she liked it

because she liked snuggling up with him on the couch and sharing a big bowl of cheese popcorn. She didn't care who won.

So when she picked teams with Ben, she always picked based on whether she'd been to their city. Or whether she wanted to go to their city. Or whether she liked the name of their city. And, of course, she always picked Minnesota because she was a Minnesotan.

Ben usually did way better than Alex. Sometimes he only got two or three wrong. But there were other times he didn't do any better than she did. So what was wrong with her way?

Finally, Ben circled Baltimore, which made Alex smile. The rest of the list went pretty fast. Ben circled Buffalo, New Orleans, and St. Louis. Then he closed his notebook.

"Okay." Ben held out his hand. "I'll read your paper now."

Alex handed it to him.

" 'Topic Sentence,' " he read aloud. " 'I'm going to be my mom's *labor coach*'?" His voice went so high it squeaked.

Kate slammed on the brakes. She whirled around. "What was that?"

"My family life project," Alex replied. "Since I can't

carry around an egg anymore, I'm going to be my mom's labor coach instead."

A car honked behind them. Kate turned back to the road. But she watched Alex in the rearview mirror as she drove. "Did your mom actually say you were going to be her labor coach?"

"Well, she's still thinking about it," Alex admitted. "But I have to turn in my topic sentence and list of sources today. Read my list of sources, Ben." She was especially proud of that.

Ben read, " 'Sources: my mom, my dad, the doctor, and the people at the hospital.' " He looked at her like she had lost her mind.

Alex ignored his look. "Mrs. Ryder only asked for three sources, but did you notice I listed four? And they're all primary sources." Alex leaned as far forward as her seat belt would allow. "Kate? If Ben asked you if he could be your labor coach, you'd say yes, wouldn't you?"

"Uh—"

"Don't worry," Ben interrupted. "I would *never* ask that!"

"But IF you asked, your mom would say yes," Alex insisted. "Wouldn't you, Kate?"

"I don't know. I'd have to think about it."

"You'd say yes," Alex said confidently as she

settled back against her seat. After all, this was a learning opportunity. And Ben's mom always said yes to learning opportunities. That was why Ben was so smart.

*　*　*

"Here's my topic sentence and list of sources." Alex handed her paper to Mrs. Ryder on her way into the classroom.

Mrs. Ryder glanced at the paper, then glared at Alex over the tops of her pointy glasses. "What kind of topic sentence is 'I'm going to be my mom's labor coach?' "

Alex swallowed. "A true one?" She hoped.

"Alexandra? Do you understand the difference between reality and fantasy?"

Alex grabbed her braid. "Yes. Reality is something that really happened. Fantasy is, well..." She was going to say fantasy was something you *want* to happen. But then Mrs. Ryder would probably say that being her mom's labor was a fantasy.

"I *am* going to be my mom's labor coach," Alex said.

Mrs. Ryder frowned. "Do you think I was born yesterday?"

No. Alex certainly didn't think that.

"No mother in her right mind would allow a child to be her labor coach. Now I want you to march down to the library and stay there until you have a suitable topic sentence and list of sources for your report."

Alex opened her mouth to argue, but then closed it when Mrs. Ryder handed her a library pass. This discussion was over.

The library was at the end of the hall. It was a big, brick room with lots of windows and beanbag chairs. Mr. Blinkman stood at the counter checking in books. He smiled when Alex came in.

Alex liked Mr. Blinkman. She liked his round glasses and his thick mustache and his dark curly hair. She also liked that he had a puzzle table in the middle of the library. Anyone who came into the library could work on the puzzle.

Alex put her library pass in the box on the counter and wandered over to the puzzle table. The puzzle with all the different kinds of candy had been finished last week, so this was a new one. Tiny pieces lay spread out all over the table. Most of the edge pieces were already put together. So was part of a snow-capped mountain. According to the empty box, this puzzle was a scene from some mountain in Austria.

Alex picked up a piece of the sky and put it into

the puzzle. Then she plopped down on one of couches and opened her notebook.

What did Mrs. Ryder mean when she said no mother would allow her child to be her labor coach? Did Mrs. Ryder actually know every single mother in the whole world? There had to be some kid *somewhere* who had been his or her mother's labor coach. Or at least a kid who had been there when his or her mom had a baby. Someone besides Olivia Greene.

What Mrs. Ryder really meant was *Alex* shouldn't be her mom's labor coach. Because Alex wasn't good enough, mature enough or responsible enough to be someone's labor coach.

Tap, tap, tap! Alex felt a finger on her shoulder.

Alex whirled around and found herself face to face with a small boy with straight dark hair. It was Ian Munk, her kindergarten buddy.

"Oh. Hi, Ian." Alex smiled real big at him.

Ian nodded, which was his way of saying hi back. Alex had never heard Ian talk out loud, but she didn't mind. Ian reminded her of Ben when Ben was little. Ben didn't talk much back then either. But Alex always knew what he wanted to say. Just like she always knew what Ian wanted to say.

Ian held up a copy of *Click, Clack, Moo.*

"Hey, that's the book I read you when our classes

got together," Alex said.

Ian nodded.

"I bet you can read that book yourself, can't you?" Alex asked.

Ian nodded again.

Alex wasn't surprised. She could tell Ian was really smart.

Hugging his book to his chest, Ian waved goodbye to Alex, then scampered off to the checkout desk. A big blond boy got in line behind him. Alex watched the blond boy warily to make sure he wasn't picking on Ian. Kids who were short and smart and quiet got picked on a lot. But the blond boy started talking to the girl behind him. Ian was okay, so Alex turned back to her notebook.

Hmm . . . what else could I do for a project besides be my mom's labor coach, she wondered. She chewed on the end of her pencil.

Her eyes drifted back to the puzzle. There was another sky piece sitting in the corner. It didn't look like there was a place for that piece yet, so she picked up the piece next to it, which looked like another mountain piece.

Alex scooted forward so she could reach the puzzle better. She found another mountain piece. And another. Before long, she had the whole top part of the mountain put together. She was just starting on the clouds when Mrs. Ryder showed up.

"The rest of the class is in the computer lab, Alexandra," she said. She said it as though that was where Alex ought to be, too.

Alex dropped the puzzle piece that was in her hand. She was sure Mrs. Ryder had said not to come back to the room until she had a new topic sentence and list of sources.

"Let's see what you've come up with," Mrs. Ryder said.

Alex chewed her bottom lip as she showed Mrs. Ryder her blank sheet of paper.

Mrs. Ryder took a deep breath in, but she never let it out.

"I'm sorry, Mrs. Ryder. I just couldn't think of anything better than a report on being my mom's labor coach."

"Then perhaps we need to call your parents in for a conference."

"Again?" Alex groaned. It had only been two weeks since the last conference.

Alex was trying. Really, she was. But every time she made the least little mistake, Mrs. Ryder got on the phone and scheduled another conference. Couldn't she ever cut Alex some slack?

24

4

Alex's foot twitched so fast it looked like it had a motor attached to it. That was what Ben always said when he saw her foot going like that.

But Ben wasn't here right now. No one was left in the classroom except Alex and Mrs. Ryder. Alex didn't like being alone in the classroom with Mrs. Ryder.

So far, all Mrs. Ryder was doing was shuffling papers on her desk. Were all those papers notes about things Alex had done wrong since their last conference? Alex knew her mom didn't like leaving her job at the day care center early to come to all these conferences. What if this conference was the final straw that convinced Mom that Alex wasn't mature enough to be there when the baby is born?

"Alexandra? ALEXANDRA!"

"What?" Alex jumped.

"I said," Mrs. Ryder began, like it was a really big deal to repeat herself. "If you want to make yourself useful, you could clean the art drawer while we wait."

"Oh. Okay." Alex slowly rose to her feet. But once she did, she realized she had to go to the bathroom. "C-could I go to the bathroom first?"

Mrs. Ryder pressed her lips together. "Apparently, you're not interested in making yourself useful."

"Yes, I am," Alex said. "I-I just have to go to the bathroom."

"Fine. Go." Mrs. Ryder waved her toward the door.

Alex sighed with relief. She hopped over Miranda's chair and scrambled to the door.

"Don't run!" Mrs. Ryder called as Alex started running down the hall.

Alex slowed to a fast walk. If she could hurry up and get done in the bathroom, maybe she'd have time to start on the art drawer. Then Mrs. Ryder would know that Alex really did want to make herself useful.

"Hey, Alex," a voice behind her called. "School's out. What are you doing still hanging around?"

Alex turned. "Ms. Westley!" she cried.

Ms. Westley was the school counselor and she was Alex's favorite person in the whole school. She had long red hair the exact same shade as Alex's. And like Alex, she wore it in a long braid down her back. But unlike Alex, Ms. Westley was really calm and wise. Alex wanted to be just like Ms. Westley when she grew up.

"How's it going?" Ms. Westley asked. Alex used to see Ms. Westley twice a week to talk about ways to control her emotions, but last year Mrs. Westley said Alex was doing better and didn't need to come anymore.

Alex looked down at the floor. "Not so great. Me and my mom and Mrs. Ryder have to have another conference today."

"How come?"

Alex shrugged. "Because I keep screwing up."

Mrs. Westley gave Alex's shoulders a squeeze. "Remember, we learn a lot more from our mistakes than we do from our successes."

If that was true, Alex would probably be a genius when she grew up because she sure made a lot of mistakes!

By the time Alex returned to her room, her mom was there. So much for cleaning out the art drawer.

Mom was sitting in Alex's desk, but she'd pushed the desk way out in front of her to make room for her huge dinosaur egg stomach, and she and Mrs. Ryder were talking about the weather. So far, Mrs. Ryder didn't look too crabby. Some of the wrinkles on her face had even disappeared.

"Oh, are you guys done with the conference?" Alex asked hopefully.

Mrs. Ryder scowled and all the wrinkles around her eyes and mouth came back. "We haven't started yet."

"No. We waited for you." Mom motioned for Alex to come over by her.

Alex did. No way was she going to sit in Reece's desk. She slid into Kaila Farrell's desk, right behind her mom.

"I suppose you're wondering why I asked you here," Mrs. Ryder said.

Alex grabbed her braid.

"Has Alexandra told you about our egg project?" Mrs. Ryder asked.

"She has."

Mrs. Ryder leaned forward like she was about to let Mom in on a big secret. "Has she also told you she broke *three* eggs?"

Alex could tell Mrs. Ryder expected Mom to say no. But Alex had no secrets. She told her mom everything.

"Yes, Alex did mention that. She also said you took her off the egg project."

"That's right," Mrs. Ryder said. She didn't even sound sorry. "Alexandra has shown she can't handle this project, so she needs to do something else for her family life unit. The problem is I can't get her to cooperate."

"Why not?" Mom cast a questioning glance at Alex.

Alex looked down at her untied shoelace.

"Well, she's convinced she's going to be your labor coach," Mrs. Ryder said with almost half a laugh.

Mom whirled around and glared at Alex. "You're telling people about this already?"

"I had to! Mrs. Ryder wanted to see my topic sentence and list of sources today."

"You mean...you're actually considering this?" Mrs. Ryder looked like she might have a heart attack or something.

"*Considering* it, yes," Mom said with a pointed glance at Alex.

"Well," Mrs. Ryder said, clearing her throat. "I hope you'll give the matter some serious thought before making a decision."

"I intend to," Mom said a little testily. "Now, about Alex's family life project—"

"What could be better than watching a baby come into the world?" Alex asked. "That's *real* family life!"

"But Alex, the baby isn't even due for six weeks," Mom said. "Your family life project must be due before that."

"It is," Mrs. Ryder said. "The family life projects are due next Friday." She smiled triumphantly.

Mom turned to Alex. "Do you have any idea what kind of report you'd like to write for this project?"

Alex shrugged. She wanted to write about seeing the baby be born.

"I've got an ultrasound scan scheduled for tomorrow morning," Mom said. "How about you come along and then you can do your report on that?"

"What's ultrasound?" Alex asked.

"It's a machine that lets us see the baby while it's inside me," Mom explained.

"Oh!" That sounded pretty good. Almost as good as seeing the baby come out. "And I'll get to miss school to go to that?" Missing school would make it even better.

"My appointment is at eight, so you won't miss too much," Mom replied.

"That sounds like a fine subject for a report," Mrs. Ryder said, folding her hands in front of her. "Can we count on you to do this, Alex?" She looked doubtful.

"I guess so."

"Good," Mrs. Ryder said. She turned to Alex's mom. "Now, as long as I have you here, Mrs. Hopewell, I'd like to talk with you privately."

Alex gulped. Why would Mrs. Ryder want to talk to Mom in private? *Now* what was she going to complain about?

Mom glanced at Alex. "Okay," she said slowly.

"You can wait out in the hallway, Alexandra." Mrs.

Ryder showed Alex to the door, then closed it firmly behind her. But Alex could still hear everything Mrs. Ryder was saying.

"I'm having a lot of trouble with Alexandra in the classroom, Mrs. Hopewell. She doesn't listen. She doesn't follow directions. I look over at her and more often than not, she's not doing what she's supposed to be doing."

"Mrs. Ryder, Alex has a central auditory processing disorder," Mom said. "She hears what you're saying, but she isn't always able to process the information. Especially if there's a lot going on around her. Remember, we talked about this at the beginning of the year."

Alex pressed her ear against to the door to hear what Mrs. Ryder said to that.

"Yes, I remember," Mrs. Ryder replied. "But I don't believe making excuses for Alexandra is helping her. She needs to listen. She needs to do her work. And she needs to control her impulses. Even if it's harder for her than it is for other kids."

Alex's eyes filled with tears. She was trying to do all that. She was trying as hard as she could.

"She's also having a hard time with her peers. She doesn't have a lot of friends."

I have Ben!

"I don't know what to say," Mom said. "I can't make kids like her. I know she's trying—"

"She's got to try harder. She won't succeed in school or in life if she doesn't learn to manage herself now."

Alex wiped her sleeve across her eyes, then moved away from the door. She didn't want to hear any more.

She went across the hall and looked at the drawings and reports on African animals that Ms. Logan's class had up on the bulletin board. Ms. Logan was the other fifth grade teacher. She was young and pretty and she smiled all the time. Even at kids who weren't in her class. Alex didn't know why she couldn't have gotten Ms. Logan for a teacher this year instead of mean old Mrs. Ryder.

A few minutes later, Mom came out of Mrs. Ryder's room. Her cheeks were red and her right eye twitched.

"Are you ready to go?" Mom asked.

Alex nodded. They started walking.

"Told you she hates me," Alex grumbled.

Mom sighed. "She doesn't understand you. That doesn't mean she hates you." Mom put her arm around Alex's shoulders and squeezed. "Look on the bright side. You've got the rest of the year to show her what a great kid you really are."

Alex stared at her mother. Who was she kidding? Alex wasn't a great kid. She'd never be a great kid. About the best she could hope for was to be a good kid. A kid who followed directions and did what she was supposed to do.

* * *

Alex was half asleep when her bedroom door opened later that night. The hall light shone on her face.

Alex opened one eye. It was her dad. He still had on his pilot's uniform.

"Dad!" Alex was instantly wide-awake. She threw off the covers and sat up. "You're home!"

Dad gave Alex a whisker rub as he hugged her. He smelled like stale airplane air and McDonald's french fries. "How's my girl?" he asked.

"Okay." Alex rubbed her eyes. "Except I broke three eggs at school. And I have to write a report. And then Mom had to have a conference with Mrs. Ryder—"

Dad pressed his finger to Alex's lips. "Shh. It's late, honey. Why don't you pick one very important thing to tell me right now. Everything else can wait until tomorrow."

Alex had no doubt what one thing on her mind

was most important. She sat up a little straighter. "Did Mom tell you I want to be there when the baby is born?"

Alex held her breath, waiting for Dad's response.

"Yes. She told me when we talked on the phone last night."

"Do you think I could? I'd listen. And I'd follow directions. I could be a big help. I could be her backup labor coach. Like if she has the baby when you're gone."

Alex's heart thumped painfully.

"Mom's not going to have the baby while I'm gone," Dad said as he gently settled Alex back against her pillow.

"She might. You never know when a baby's going to come."

"True. But I won't be flying the week before she's due. And the baby will probably come late rather than early. You were a whole two weeks late."

"I could still help you be Mom's labor coach. Like if you need a break or something."

"I don't know, Alex. Your mom and I need to talk about it some more. And you," Dad paused to pull the quilt up to Alex's chin, "need to get some sleep."

"Okay," Alex said, showing how agreeable and cooperative she really was. She hunkered down under her covers. "I'm glad you're home, Dad."

"Me too, honey." Dad smiled at Alex like she was the whole reason he came home.

5

"Mrs. Hopewell?" a voice called. Alex bounced out of her chair. "That's us!" she told her mom and dad, in case they weren't paying attention.

The woman who'd called them smiled as she held the door open. She wore black glasses that were about five times the size of her eyes. Her nametag read MONICA.

"Go right in," Monica said.

Alex did. "Hey. It's kind of dark in here." She flipped the switch and bright light from the overhead fixture filled the small room.

Monica switched the light back off. "We can see better without that light," she said, letting the door close softly behind her. Fortunately, the black and white TV on Monica's desk gave off enough light that they could find their way in the small room.

"You can lie down over there, Mrs. Hopewell." Monica pointed to the examining table in the middle of the room.

"Why don't you and I sit down over here so we're out of the way." Dad steered Alex to two chairs over by the wall.

Alex watched as Monica lifted Mom's shirt. Whoa! If Alex thought her mom's stomach was big before, it looked even bigger without a shirt hanging down over it.

"Are you *sure* the baby's not going to come for six weeks?" Alex asked.

"That's why we're here," Mom said. "I've grown a lot in the last couple of weeks, so the doctor wants to see how big the baby is."

Monica squirted a clear gel onto Mom's stomach. "Brr! That's cold!" Mom shivered as Monica took something that looked like a microphone and smeared the gel around.

The microphone was attached to the TV on the desk. Monica kept glancing at the TV over her shoulder, but there wasn't anything to see.

"It looks like you're on the wrong channel," Alex said, trying to be helpful.

Monica smiled. "It does look like a TV that's not working too well, doesn't it?" She moved the microphone around Mom's stomach as she talked. "But actually it's a computer. And this," she nodded toward the microphone, "is a scanner. It uses sound waves to produce a picture of the baby."

"You mean it listens for the baby's crying?"

"Not exactly," Monica said. "This machine sends out sound waves, and the sound waves reflect off the baby. The computer takes those sound waves and translates them into pictures we can see."

Alex stared at the screen. She didn't get it. How could sound waves make a picture? Obviously they didn't make a very good picture because Alex couldn't see a thing. It was like last summer when the cable went out and they couldn't get any channels on TV.

"This right here," Monica pointed to a blob on the screen, "is your mom's bladder."

Alex took a polite look. But bladders weren't very interesting.

"And *this* is your baby brother or sister."

"Where?" Alex leaned forward.

"Right there." Dad pointed. He held her close to him and rested his whiskery chin on her shoulder. "Don't you see that big round ball? I think that's the baby's head."

"That's right." Monica swiveled around. "You can come over here if you want to get a better look," she told Alex.

"Okay!" Alex stepped around the table and went to stand behind Monica.

"See this right here?" Monica traced a line on the screen with her finger. "This is the baby's forehead and nose and chin."

"How can you tell?"

"Years of practice," Monica said. She wrote some numbers down on the paper in front of her.

Alex stared at the screen until she thought her eyes would bug out. "Oh!" she cried suddenly. "I think I see it. There," she pointed. "That's its nose and that's its mouth."

"Yep!" Monica smiled at Alex.

"It's sort of like one of those 3-D hidden pictures," Alex said.

"Sort of." Monica moved the microphone on Mom's stomach and the picture changed. "There's an arm," she said. "And the legs."

Alex could make out the arm, but not the legs.

"Would you like to know the baby's sex?" Monica asked Mom and Dad.

"You can tell *that?*" Alex cried.

"Sometimes," Monica replied. "It depends on whether the baby cooperates. This baby is being very cooperative at the moment, so I could tell you with about a 99% certainty what it is."

"Oh yes! Tell us!" Alex rocked back and forth from her toes to her heels. "Please tell us!"

"No, no, no!" Mom said, waving her hand. "I don't want to know. Not until it's born."

Was Mom crazy?

"Why not?" Alex asked.

"I want to be surprised."

"Can't you be surprised right now?" Alex asked. "What's the difference if you find out today or when the baby's born?"

"I could ask *you* the same question," Mom replied.

Alex groaned.

"I used that same argument on your mom when she was pregnant with you." Dad tugged on Alex's braid. "And I can tell you it's no use. If your mom doesn't want to know, you're not going to be able to change her mind."

Alex scowled. But then she got an idea. "Maybe Monica could tell me what it is and I could tell you. But we'll keep it a secret from Mom so she can still be surprised."

Monica smiled. "Sorry. I can only tell if your mom wants me to."

"And I don't want you to," Mom said firmly.

"Darn."

Monica moved a dial and the picture on the screen changed. "There you can see the baby's heart beating," she said. "It looks good and strong."

Monica changed the picture several more times, took some notes, then set the scanner down. "That's it for today, Mrs. Hopewell." She handed Mom a tissue to wipe the goop off her stomach.

"What did you think, Alex?" Dad asked as Monica turned on the lights.

Alex shrugged. "It was okay."

"Just okay?" Mom sat up and Monica helped her down from the table.

"Well, I thought I'd be able to see what the baby really looked like. And I wish I could tell whether the baby was a boy or a girl."

"You'll find that out when it's born," Mom said

Alex sighed. That was a long time to wait.

* * *

Mom and Dad didn't take Alex to school right away when the ultrasound appointment was over. First they went over to Perkins for breakfast. Mom and Dad both ordered bacon and eggs. Alex ordered a blueberry muffin.

"So." Mom folded her hands on the table once the waitress was gone. "We need to talk about whether we're going to let Alex be there when the baby is born."

Alex sat up a little straighter to show her mom and dad how mature and responsible she was.

Dad took a sip of coffee. "Believe me, Alex. There's nothing more amazing than seeing a baby come into the world. But sitting at the hospital, waiting for the baby to come, is not easy."

"What do you mean?" Alex asked.

"He means it takes a long time for a baby to be born," Mom explained. "A really long time. I was in labor with you for almost eighteen hours. There's nothing to do in the hospital. You can't be running around—"

"I wouldn't be running around," Alex protested. "I'd be helping!"

"Helping how?" Dad scratched his beard.

Alex shrugged. "However you wanted me to. I could get Mom water, fluff her pillow, tell her to breathe." What else did the people do on TV?

"For eighteen hours?" Dad asked.

Alex looked down at the table. "You don't think I can do it. You don't think I can be calm and follow directions."

Mom and Dad exchanged a look. Then Dad reached across the table for Alex's hand. "I'm an adult and it's hard for me to sit in the hospital with your mother. I can't imagine what it would be like for you."

"Having a baby isn't like it looks on TV," Mom said.

"That's right," Dad added. "Your mom's going to be in a lot of pain. You'll hear sounds come out of her that you've never heard before and you'll never hear again." Mom frowned and slapped him on the arm when he said that, but he just grinned at her, rubbed his arm and continued, "She's going to be working through those contractions and I'm going to have to help her."

"And I can't be worrying about what you're doing, whether you're getting into trouble," Mom said.

"I won't get into trouble!" Alex cried. "Really, I won't!"

Mom and Dad exchanged another look.

"I like the idea of all of us being there when the baby is born," Mom said. "But I just don't know whether it's the right thing."

It is! Alex thought. It's *definitely the right thing.* But how could she convince her parents of that?

"Well, why don't we think about it a little bit more," Dad said as the waitress brought their food. "We don't need to make a decision today."

"Okay," Mom said.

Alex sighed. If they weren't going to make a decision today, when *would* they?

6

"With ultrasound you can see a baby's inside and its outside, even whether it has a—" Alex clamped her hand over her mouth. One time Justin said the word "penis" out loud and Mrs. Ryder sent him to Mr. Mallett's office.

"Has a what?" Miranda asked.

Mrs. Ryder's eyes bore into Alex like laser guns. She probably knew exactly what word Alex was thinking and she was just waiting for Alex to say it so she could yell at her.

Well, Alex wasn't falling for it. "You can see whether the baby is a boy or a girl," she said as she glanced over at Mrs. Ryder.

If Mrs. Ryder noticed Alex had found a better way to say it, she didn't show it. She still looked like she'd just swallowed a big old Brussels sprout.

"So, what is it?" Ben asked as Drew passed Alex's ultrasound photo to him.

"What's what?"

"The baby! Is your mom having a boy or a girl?"

"Oh. I don't know. My mom didn't want the lady to

tell us. She wants to be surprised."

"Are you really going to be there when your mom's baby is born, Alex?" Kaila asked.

"Yes!" Alex said right away. But then she noticed Mrs. Ryder standing there with her arms crossed. "I mean," Alex corrected herself. "My parents and I talked about it this morning and—"

"And they said yes?" Miranda looked surprised.

"Well, they're still thinking about it," Alex admitted.

"They better think long and hard," Reece put in. "Can you imagine Alex Hopeless in the delivery room?" He made his voice all high and squeaky. "Get out of my way, doctor. I'm Alex Hopeless and I want to help. Oops. I didn't mean to drop the baby on its head."

Everyone laughed.

"Reece," Mrs. Ryder warned.

Alex could feel her blood vessels bulging with anger. "I wouldn't drop a baby on its head!" she cried.

"Right," Reece said with a smirk.

"I wouldn't!"

"Okay, that's enough," Mrs. Ryder said. By this time, the ultrasound photo had made its way all around the classroom. Mrs. Ryder picked it up from Holly Farrington and returned it to Alex. "I think that's enough talk about your mother's pregnancy.

Right now it's time for math."

* * *

"I don't know," Ben said on the way home from school. "It could be a boy." He held the ultrasound photo up to the sun and squinted at it. "That could be a penis right there."

Alex looked. "No, I think that's a leg."

"I thought this was a leg over here."

"That's the other leg."

Ben handed the photo back to Alex. "I give up. I can't tell what anything is on here."

Alex held the photo up to the sun and looked again. She could make out the head real good. And one arm. But the rest was pretty fuzzy.

"What are you guys looking at?" Olivia Greene called from across the street. As usual, she had on a cotton dress with no shoes or socks. She was sitting on her bike, her bare toes pressed into the sidewalk for balance.

"It's my mom's ultrasound photo," Alex called back.

"Oh, can I see?" Olivia begged.

Alex and Ben exchanged a look. They usually tried not to spend a lot of time with Olivia. She was just so weird. But Olivia *had* seen her sister's birth,

46

Alex reminded herself. Maybe she knew something about ultrasound photos?

Alex crossed the street, then held the photo up so Olivia could see it. "We're trying to tell whether my mom's baby is going to be a boy or a girl," she explained.

Olivia squinted at the photo. Her long brown hair fanned out around her shoulders.

"What do you think?" Alex asked. "Can you tell whether it's a boy or a girl?"

"Not from this." Olivia handed the photo back to Alex.

"Darn." Alex slipped the photo inside the envelope it came in.

"I know another way to tell, though," Olivia said mysteriously as she pushed her bike along beside Alex and Ben.

"You do? How?"

"Go get your mom's wedding ring and I'll show you."

Alex's mom was at work. But her mom's wedding ring was on her dresser. Alex knew it was there because her mom had complained her fingers were swelling so much she couldn't wear it anymore.

"I don't know." Alex grabbed her braid. "I don't think my mom would want me to take her ring."

"Why not?" Olivia asked. "We won't hurt it any."

Alex bit her lip. "What are you going to do with it?"

"I'm going to put it on a string, hold it real still and see which way it turns," Olivia replied.

That didn't sound too bad.

"If the ring turns to the right, your mom's going to have a girl," Olivia explained. "If it turns to the left, she's going to have a boy."

"Really?" Alex asked.

Ben burst out laughing. "You can't tell whether a baby's going to be a boy or a girl by which direction the mom's wedding ring turns!"

"You can, too!" Olivia looked mad. "Go get your mom's ring and I'll prove it."

They were only going to need the ring for a couple of minutes, then Alex could put it right back. "Okay," Alex said. "I'll go get it."

"I'll get some string." Olivia turned her bike around.

Alex took off for home.

"Wait, Alex!" Ben called after her.

"What?"

"I thought we were going over to my house to play computer games."

"We will," Alex promised. "But first I want to find

out whether my mom's having a boy or a girl."

"She's going to have a *cow* if she catches you stealing her wedding ring!"

"I'm not stealing it," Alex said. "I'm just...borrowing it. I'll put it right back."

"Sure, whatever," Ben said. He clearly thought it was a bad idea.

Alex took her front steps two at a time and banged the front door open. "Hello?" she called. No response.

There was a note on the kitchen table from Alex's dad that said he'd gone golfing.

Good! That meant Alex was home alone.

She raced up the stairs and into her parents' bedroom. Her mom's wedding ring was exactly where she expected it to be — inside the small china box on Mom's dresser. Alex hesitated just for a second. Then she grabbed the ring and hurried down the stairs and out the door.

Olivia was waiting across the street, twirling a piece of string around her finger. Ben just stood there shaking his head.

"Okay, give me the ring." Olivia held out her hand.

Alex handed her the ring. Her heart thumped as she watched Olivia tie the string around it.

"Be careful," Alex said. "That ring belonged to my dad's grandma."

"Don't be such a worry wart," Olivia said. She acted like she was older than Alex rather than younger. "The knot is really tight. See?"

Alex tugged on the ring. It didn't come loose. "Okay," she said, satisfied.

"Are you hoping for a boy or a girl?" Olivia asked. She flipped her hair behind her shoulder.

"A boy." Except for Reece, Alex seemed to get along better with boys than she did with girls.

"I think it's going to be a girl," Olivia said as she held the string up and let the ring dangle.

All three of them stared at the ring. It didn't move.

"It's not doing anything," Ben said finally. "Just wait," Olivia said. "It'll start turning soon."

Alex held her breath as she stared at the ring. *Left,* she thought. *Go to the left.*

Slowly, the ring twisted to the left.

"Yes!" Alex cried, jumping up and down. "It's a boy!"

"Wait. It's not done," Olivia said.

Alex watched as the ring suddenly switched direction. Now it was twisting to the right. "See, it's a girl!" Olivia grinned.

Alex frowned. "But it was a boy two minutes ago!"

"And now it's a girl." Olivia shrugged.

"I told you this wouldn't work," Ben said.

Alex bit her lip. "It might be working," she said. She didn't want to give up. "Maybe my mom's having twins. A boy and a girl."

"If she was, you would've seen two babies on the ultrasound," Ben said.

"Maybe we should try it again." Olivia grabbed the ring to stop its turning, then held it straight once more.

But before it turned in either direction, Alex noticed a car. Her mom's car. It was just pulling into the driveway across the street.

What was she doing home already?

Was there time to grab the ring and run it back to the little box on Mom's dresser before she noticed it was gone? Probably not. Mom would wonder where Alex was going in such a hurry.

No, Alex was better off staying here. Mom probably wouldn't walk all the way over here. She'd just wave at her, then go inside.

But Mom *did* walk over. "Hi, guys," she said. "What are you doing?"

Alex grabbed her braid. She looked down at her dirty tennis shoes. Her heart was pounding so hard she could practically taste it in the back of her throat.

"We're trying to see whether you're having a boy or a girl," Olivia said cheerfully.

"Oh? And how are you doing that?"

Mom drew in her breath. Apparently, she had just *seen* how they were doing that.

"Is that my wedding ring?" Mom's fingers tightened on Alex's shoulder blades.

Alex gulped. "Sort of," she said as she chewed on her braid. She chewed so hard she could taste the apple shampoo she'd used two nights ago.

"May I have it, please?" Mom held out her hand and Olivia handed it over, string and all.

"Thank you," she told Olivia through angry teeth. "Come on, Alex." She grabbed Alex's arm and steered her towards home.

Uh oh. Alex was in big trouble now.

"Maybe we can try again later," Olivia called after her.

"Don't count on it." Ben cleared his throat. "I'll see you tomorrow, Alex."

Mom turned around and glared at him and Olivia.

"Or uh, maybe I'll see you on Monday instead," Ben said.

"What were you thinking?" Mom asked once they were inside their house.

"I just wanted to know whether the baby was a boy or girl," Alex said. She plopped down on the living room couch and hugged her knees to her chest. She hated it when people got mad at her. She just hated it.

"Do you really think swinging my wedding ring around in circles would tell you that?"

Alex shrugged. "Olivia said it would."

Mom gave Alex her you-should-know-better look. "That ring belonged to your father's grandmother. I can't believe you'd take it without my permission."

"I wish I hadn't taken it," Alex mumbled, tracing her finger over a blue thread in the couch.

"So do I. I'm really disappointed in you, Alex. I thought you were making better decisions now that you're in fifth grade."

"I'm sorry," Alex said in a small voice. She thought she was making better decisions, too.

Did this mean Mom and Dad weren't going to let her be there when the baby was born?

Alex was afraid to ask.

1

"What if my mom says no?" Alex asked on Monday morning when she and Ben walked to school. "What if she says I can't be there when the baby's born?"

Ben shrugged. "Then I guess you'll see the baby after it's born, like every other kid whose mom has a baby."

But Alex didn't want to be like every other kid. Not about this. She wanted to see a baby be born.

"Ben? Do you think a kid like me could grow up and be a doctor who delivers babies?"

Ben straightened his glasses. "What do you mean a kid like you?"

"You know. A kid who's not very smart."

"You're smart," Ben said.

Alex kicked a pebble on the sidewalk. It was nice of Ben to say that, but she knew it wasn't true. Smart people did well in school. They followed directions. They got along with other people. They made good decisions.

"There's lots of different kinds of smart," Ben said. "I'm school smart. But you're..." Ben paused.

"I'm what?" What kind of smart was she?

But before Ben could answer, Reece Burmeister skidded to a stop behind Alex. "Eeeeeek!" he screamed in Alex's ear. "It's my ex-wife, Alex Hopeless!"

Alex glared at him. "Go away, Reece," she warned. "I'm not in the mood."

But instead of going away, Reece hopped off his bike and walked alongside her. "Not in the mood for what?" he asked. "All I want to do is have you say hi to little Eggbert here." He carefully picked up his egg from the milk carton basket he'd hung over the handlebars of his bike.

Alex stared at the egg. Reece had taken a fat purple magic marker and drawn huge buggy eyes, a pointed nose and a smile with buckteeth on it.

"Why did you make him look so ugly?" Alex wrinkled her nose.

"Ugly!" Reece looked offended. "That's a terrible thing to say about your child."

"He's not *my* child. Mrs. Ryder gave him to you, not me."

"She just gave me *custody* of him. You're still his real mother."

Alex sniffed. She didn't even have visiting rights.

"What was that, Eggbert?" Reece held the egg to his ear. "Yes, son. I'm afraid this terrible person is your real mom. She's the one who killed your three brothers."

Alex's jaw dropped open. "I did not," she cried. She wasn't sure who she was talking to—Reece or the ugly, purple egg.

"But then Judge Ryder decided your mom was unfit to raise children," Reece went on. "So she gave you to me."

"Stop it," Alex warned.

"Come on, Alex." Ben touched her arm. "Let's go."

"If you see her coming," Reece shook his finger at the egg. "I want you to cross the street. You'll be safer crossing the street by yourself than walking past her."

"I said, 'stop it!' " Alex reached out and gave Reece a shove. It wasn't a very hard shove, but for some reason, Reece lost his balance. He fell into his bike and both he and the bike crashed to the ground.

"Oh no," Ben moaned as he slapped his forehead.

Alex gasped as egg yolk dripped from Reece's pants onto the sidewalk. Pieces of shell were still clenched in his fist.

At first Reece just sat there. Then he raised his eyes. "Look what you did!" he yelled, waving the broken egg shells at her.

Alex took a step back.

"You killed *another* one!" Reece wiped the egg yolk

onto his jeans.

"N-n-no, I didn't," Alex argued. "I didn't even touch him."

"No, but you touched me." Reece climbed to his feet. "You pushed me and knocked him out of my hand." A slow smile spread across Reece's face. "Wait until Mrs. Ryder hears about this."

Alex gulped. Great. Just what she needed. More trouble with Mrs. Ryder.

"Come on, Alex." Ben tugged at Alex's jacket sleeve. "Let's just go."

Reece picked up his bike and swung his leg over the back of it. "You're in trouble," he sang as he sailed past Alex and Ben.

Alex felt like grabbing a handful of stones from the nearby flowerbed and hurling them at Reece's back. She wanted to hurt Reece. She wanted to hurt him bad.

"Don't do it," Ben said suddenly.

Alex stared at Ben. The two of them had known each other their whole lives, but she never realized he could actually read her mind.

"Whatever you're thinking, don't do it," Ben said. "It's not worth it. Reece loves to make you mad. He loves to get you in trouble."

"Tell me about it." Half the time Alex got in

trouble, it was because of Reece.

"So, don't let him do it," Ben said.

Alex snorted. "How am I supposed to stop him?" That was like asking the earth to stop rotating.

"Just ignore him. When he starts teasing you, ignore him."

That would be the smart thing to do, Alex thought. The only problem was Reece was impossible to ignore.

* * *

Mrs. Ryder was writing the day's schedule on the board when Alex walked in. Reece was sitting at his desk, one ankle resting over the opposite knee. An evil smile spread across his face when he saw Alex. He popped up out of his seat, marched up to Mrs. Ryder and showed her his empty egg basket.

"It was Alex's fault," Reece said right away. "She pushed me and I fell and Eggbert got broken."

Mrs. Ryder sighed and raised her eyes to the ceiling.

"He started it!" Alex tried to defend herself. "He was bugging me!"

But Mrs. Ryder didn't want to hear it. "You need to stop blaming others for your actions, Alexandra, and take some responsibility for yourself."

What? Alex dropped her backpack with the thud. "But what about Reece? Doesn't he have to take responsibility, too?"

"Alexandra," Mrs. Ryder said in a warning voice.

Alex clamped her teeth together. She was arguing again, but she couldn't help it. Mrs. Ryder had barely said a word to Reece. How come other kids could do the exact same thing she had done and not get in any trouble, but any time she did something wrong, look out! And if Alex tried to say anything about the unfairness of it all, she only got in more trouble.

The bell rang and Mrs. Ryder motioned for Alex and Reece to sit down. Mrs. Ryder never did say anything else to Reece about his broken egg. She just took roll and lunch count, then she reminded everyone that today was the day they were supposed to go and read to their kindergarten buddies.

Drew waved his hand in the air. "Are we supposed to bring our egg babies?"

"Of course," Mrs. Ryder said. "They go everywhere you go."

"But what if the kindergarteners break them?" Miranda asked nervously.

"They won't," Mrs. Ryder replied. "The kindergarteners are very interested in our project. So before you start reading, you can share a little of what we've been doing. Those of you who don't have eggs," Mrs. Ryder glanced pointedly at Alex, "can explain to your buddies why you don't have an egg."

Reece raised his hand. "Mrs. Ryder? Do you think it's a good idea for Alex to go to Mrs. Jackson's room? I mean, what if she kills her kindergarten buddy?"

Everyone laughed.

Alex scowled. "Very funny."

"Reece," Mrs. Ryder said in a tired voice. "You're not being helpful. Okay, everyone. Line up." Mrs. Ryder turned off the lights, then they all trooped down to Mrs. Jackson's room.

Alex saw Ian sitting up straight in a red beanbag chair over by the windows. He was reading *Click, Clack, Moo.* There was another book on the floor beside him.

"Hi, Ian," she said as she moved the book on the floor and plopped down.

Ian held up his hand in greeting. He was still reading.

Alex glanced around the room and saw all the other kids clustered in small groups here and there. They were all talking about the eggs. Kaila and Stafford even let their kindergarten buddies hold their egg. But Miranda kept a firm grip on her and Ben's egg.

Alex turned back to Ian. "You're probably wondering what all those other kids are talking about."

Ian closed his book and looked at her expectantly.

"We've been carrying around eggs in Mrs. Ryder's room. We're supposed to pretend the eggs are our babies. Only me and Reece don't have one. We broke ours. You can go look at someone else's egg if you want, though." Alex didn't want Ian to miss out on what all the other kids were doing.

Ian craned his neck so he could get a look at Kaila and Stafford's egg, then he sat back as though he'd seen all he needed to see.

"Are you sure?" Alex asked.

Ian nodded solemnly. Then he sort of raised his eyebrow at Alex. He had kind of a worried look on his face.

"You want to know whether I got in trouble?" Alex asked.

Ian nodded.

"Well, sort of. But it's not that big of a deal. They were just eggs. They weren't real babies." Alex didn't want Ian to worry about her.

She leaned closer to him. "You want me to tell you a secret? My mom's having a baby and I'm going to be there when it's born."

Ian's eyes got really big.

"I'm going to help out in the delivery room. I'm going to cut the umbilical cord. And when I grow up, I'm going to be a doctor and deliver babies every day," Alex said.

"I might deliver babies, too," Ian said.

Now Alex's eyes were big. Ian had talked! Alex had known Ian for two months and he *never* talked. But he talked today.

It was probably best not to make a big deal about it. Alex cleared her throat. "Really?" she said as though it was perfectly normal for him to talk.

Ian nodded. "Or maybe I'll deliver pizzas instead." Then he handed Alex his book. He was ready for her to start reading.

* * *

"I talked to Dr. Anneling about you wanting to be there when the baby is born," Mom announced at dinner that night.

Alex just about dropped the bowl of mashed potatoes she was passing to her dad. Fortunately, Dad grabbed it in time.

"What did she say?" Alex asked.

"She said I wasn't the first to ask such a thing. Apparently she's had other kids there while their moms had babies."

Alex *knew* she wasn't the first to come up with the idea.

"So, she thinks it's okay?" Dad asked.

Mom dabbed the corner of her mouth with her napkin. "She said it depends on the kid. She's had four-year-olds who could handle it and ten-year-olds who couldn't. She says it's up to us."

"I can handle it," Alex said. She felt like bouncing in her chair, but she stopped herself. "Really, I can!"

"Dr. Anneling suggested we set up a time we can get together at the hospital. She wants to meet Alex and show her around. She's also got a movie Alex can watch."

"What kind of movie?" Alex asked.

"A movie on childbirth," Mom replied. "That way you can see what you're getting into and you can ask questions."

Alex only had one question. "When do we get to do this?"

"Tuesday after school," Mom said.

Alex could hardly wait!

8

Ben had tae kwon do after school on Mondays, so Alex walked home from school alone. Olivia was playing hopscotch across the street while Mrs. Greene sat on their front step rocking Olivia's baby sister, Grace.

"Hey, Alex!" Olivia called, her hands straight out at her sides as she balanced on one bare foot. "Do you want to play hopscotch?"

Alex didn't. Not really. But Ben wasn't around. Alex's mom was at the day care center and her dad was probably flying over Cleveland or Cincinnati

"For a little while, I guess," Alex called back. She dropped her book bag on her own front porch, then skipped across the street.

When she got there she realized Mrs. Greene wasn't just rocking Grace. She was *breastfeeding* her. Right there on her front step.

Mrs. Greene had a blanket draped over her shoulder and the baby, but Alex knew what was going on under there. She wondered how breastfeeding worked. How did the milk get in a lady's breast? And how did the baby get it out?

"Are you going to play?" Olivia held a rock out to Alex.

Alex took it. She tossed it down on the first hop-scotch square and took her turn, all the while keeping one eye focused on Mrs. Greene and Grace.

When Alex jumped off the hopscotch board, Olivia took her turn. By then Grace had finished eating. Mrs. Greene held the baby against her shoulder and burped her.

It had been a long time since Alex had seen Olivia's baby sister. She had really pudged out. It was like someone had stuck a hose in her and blown up her arms and legs. But Alex knew it wouldn't be polite to say that, so when Mrs. Greene caught her staring, she just said, "Grace is getting really big."

"Yes. She's five months old today," Mrs. Greene said as Grace let out a whopper of a burp. "Your mom's going to be having her baby soon, too, isn't she?"

"Not for another month. I get to be there when the baby's born."

"Really?" Mrs. Greene said. She acted like it was no big deal. Like being there when your baby brother or sister is born was a normal thing to do.

"My mom's having her baby in the hospital, though, not at home. But I still get to be there."

The more Alex said it out loud, the more she believed it.

"Good for you, Alex." Mrs. Greene smiled. "I think having the whole family there to share in the birth experience brings everyone closer together." She sat Grace on her lap so Grace could see what Alex and Olivia were doing. Grace waved her little hands around and smiled.

Alex smiled back. She couldn't resist reaching out and twisting her finger through Grace's fine, brown curls and then touching her smooth baby cheek. Babies' skin was so amazingly soft.

"Would you like to hold her, Alex?"

Alex stared at Mrs. Greene. "Really?" Alex had never held a real live baby before.

"Sure. Just sit down on the step."

Alex wanted to. She *really* wanted to. But what if she dropped Grace? Or did something else wrong?

"Sit down," Mrs. Greene said again, patting the spot beside her on the step.

Alex sat. Then Mrs. Greene carefully set Grace on Alex's lap.

"Oh wow," Alex breathed. Grace was like a big baby doll. Only she was softer. And heavier. And she had an interesting smell. Like baby powder and sour milk mixed together.

Grace looked at Alex like "who are you and what am I doing on your lap?" But she didn't cry. Alex bounced her knees a little and Grace smiled. She had two bottom teeth.

"Mom, you said we could make carob cookies today," Olivia said in a whiny voice. Her long brown hair blew in the breeze. "Can we do that now? Can Alex help?"

"Sure," Mrs. Greene said. "Would you like to make carob cookies with us, Alex?"

"What's carob?"

"It's a chocolate substitute. It's much better for you than chocolate. We don't use sugar in our cookies either. So these cookies are actually quite healthy."

Alex tried not to wrinkle her nose. In her opinion, if you were going to make cookies, you should make real cookies. With sugar and chocolate and other stuff that's bad for you. Otherwise why bother?

"I better not. My mom doesn't like me to snack, even on healthy stuff, too close to supper," Alex said. Which was sort of the truth.

"You don't have to eat any right now. You could bring some home and eat them for dessert," Olivia said.

Grace started fussing a little, so Mrs. Greene took her back.

"No, I should probably go. I've got homework."
Also true.

"Darn," Olivia said.

* * *

On Tuesday Alex had a hard time concentrating at school. She just kept staring at the clock, watching the minutes tick by, waiting for school to get out. After school, Alex and her mom were going over to the hospital to talk to Dr. Anneling about Alex being there when the baby was born.

Tuesday was D-Day. Decision Day. Alex really wanted to make a good impression.

Alex had unbraided her hair this morning, brushed it until it shined, then rebraided it and tied it with a brand new bow. She had put on a flouncy white shirt and her brand new jeans. She didn't even play soccer or kickball during the morning recess because she didn't want to take a chance on getting dirty.

Her mom was picking her up right after school and they were going right to the hospital from there. There wouldn't be time to stop home and change clothes.

I have to remember to walk slow and be polite, Alex told herself during math. *Don't run. Don't be loud. In fact, don't talk at all unless Dr. Anneling talks to you. Remember to say please and thank you—*

"ALEXANDRA!"

"What?" Alex jumped.

The whole class was staring at her.

Ben and Kaila were at the board. Mrs. Ryder was glaring at Alex and holding out a piece of chalk to her.

"Problem three?" Mrs. Ryder said it like she'd already asked Alex ten times to go do problem three on the board.

Alex swallowed. Maybe Mrs. Ryder *had* asked her ten times? She dragged herself up out of her seat and went to get the chalk.

"You'll need your worksheet," Mrs. Ryder said.

Alex turned around and grabbed her worksheet. Unfortunately, she hadn't exactly gotten to problem three yet. In fact, she hadn't exactly gotten to any of the problems yet. That was because the whole sheet was story problems. Alex wasn't good at story problems. She was pretty good at math, but lousy at story problems. It was too hard to find the math in all those words.

Alex picked up the chalk and read the problem to herself. *George and his brother Bill each have a paper route. If George can deliver 45 newspapers in 30 minutes and Bill can deliver 25 newspapers in 15 minutes, which boy will deliver the most newspapers in an hour?*

First of all, Alex thought, wouldn't that depend on where they're delivering the newspapers? If the houses where George delivered were really close together and he didn't have to go up and down a lot of steps, he'd probably be able to deliver his papers faster than Bill. But if the houses were really far apart, and it took a long time to get from one house to another, then Bill would probably be faster. Or if George had a bike and Bill didn't, that would make a difference. Or if Bill's mom drove him in her car. And why were both these newspaper carriers boys? Alex wondered. Girls had paper routes, too!

"Alexandra," Mrs. Ryder interrupted Alex's thinking. "You haven't written anything yet."

"That's because—"

Bzzt! Bzzt! Bzzt! Alex jumped and both the worksheet and the chalk slipped from her fingers.

"Fire drill!" several kids shouted out.

Everyone jumped up out of their seats.

Bzzt! Bzzt! Bzzt!

Alex cupped her hands over her ears. That loud noise pulsed in her head. It made her feel like her head was going to explode. She had to get out. Away from the noise.

"No running!" Mrs. Ryder shouted above the noise. "Everybody line up. Then *walk* in an orderly fashion down the middle stairs and out to the playground."

Bzzt! Bzzt! Bzzt!

Alex tried to walk in an orderly fashion. She tried not to push Justin, who shuffled along at a snail's pace in front of her. But she had to get away from that non-stop buzzing. It hurt her head. It hurt her ears.

"I don't know why we have to walk in such a straight line," Justin said once they burst through the doors into the October sunshine.

Relief. The buzzing wasn't so loud out here.

"Do you think if there was really a fire we'd walk in a straight line?" Justin asked.

"No," Alex said. The buzzing had stopped, but kids from the other classes were still streaming through the doors. "If there was a real fire, everyone would be running and pushing and screaming."

"Hey, Ben," Drew said. "Why do you have your math book?"

Alex turned. Ben held his math book against his hip.

He blushed. "I don't know. I just grabbed it when the fire alarm went off."

"You're only supposed to grab stuff that's really important," Stafford said.

"Yeah, dude. Let the math book burn," Drew added.

Everyone laughed. Even Ben.

Alex glanced around to see what other people had brought outside. Miranda had her little soup can bed with the baby egg inside hung over her wrist.

The baby eggs!

"Hey," Alex cried. "Did you all remember to grab your baby eggs?"

"No, I left mine on my desk," Kaila said.

"Me too," Melanie said.

"You left your baby eggs inside a burning building?" Alex exclaimed.

"It's just a fire drill, Alex," said Melanie. "Chill out!"

But it wasn't just a fire drill. You were supposed to pretend the fire drill was real and the school was really on fire and you had to get out.

And the egg babies weren't just eggs. You were supposed to pretend they were real. Real babies.

You wouldn't leave a real baby inside a burning building. You wouldn't even leave a real baby inside a building while you went outside in an orderly fashion for a fire drill.

Alex took off running toward the school.

"Where are you going, Alex?" somebody yelled after her.

But Alex didn't stop to answer. She just kept running.

A couple of teachers were standing by the big double doors talking to Mr. Mallett. Alex ran right on past them.

"Hey!" Mr. Mallett cried. "Where are you going? The bell hasn't rung yet. You can't go inside."

But Alex was already inside. "I have to get the babies," she called over her shoulder. She took the stairs two at a time.

She wondered just how many baby eggs had been left on desks. Abandoned. Forgotten.

"Come back here!" a voice demanded. Then Alex heard footsteps pounding up the stairs.

"I just have to get the babies," she said again. She was doing the right thing. She knew she was.

Alex opened the door to her classroom. The lights were out, but she could see perfectly. She could hardly believe it. Most of the kids had left their egg babies sitting on their desks.

Could Alex actually carry all those egg babies herself?

Well, she'd have to put several in each container. People could sort them out later.

She snatched up the small square box bed from the desk that was closest to her. Quickly she made her way up and down the aisles, filling the box with as many egg babies as she dared.

Somebody in the hallway rushed past Mrs. Ryder's room.

Alex continued up and down the aisles. When her first box was full, she grabbed another container. Then another.

Mrs. Ryder would be so amazed. Alex had gone back inside and saved all the egg babies. After everyone else had forgotten them.

See. Alex was *responsible.* She just rescued seventeen eggs. Juggling four full containers of eggs, Alex hurried out into the hallway, down the stairs and back outside.

The bell rang and Alex jumped. She wanted to cover her ears, but her hands were full, so she just grit her teeth. And once the bell stopped ringing, Alex ran toward the kids in her class, who were gathering on the blacktop in front of the monkey bars.

Other classes were making their way to the door, but Alex kept her eyes on her own class as she hurried toward them.

"Look, everyone!" she called, waving her four containers as she dodged all the kids who were trying to come inside. "I saved your egg babies! I saved your egg babies!"

Mrs. Ryder stepped out from behind a crowd and Alex skidded to a stop. But she didn't get stopped fast enough.

She rammed the soup can bed and the cottage cheese carton bed into Mrs. Ryder's stomach. The two box beds slipped out of her hands and hit the ground.

Splat!

Both Alex and Mrs. Ryder were covered with broken egg guts.

* * *

Alex tried to clean the egg guts off her flouncy shirt and new jeans, but she couldn't get it all. She was afraid that if she stayed in the bathroom much longer, Mrs. Ryder would really get mad. So she slowly dragged herself back to her class.

Everybody glared at Alex when she came in.

All the egg babies were gone except for the one Miranda had carried outside. The egg project was over.

"Obviously this was a bad idea," Mrs. Ryder said. The little blue vein at the edge of her forehead pulsed.

Nobody moved. It was so quiet in Mrs. Ryder's room that you could hear the wind whistling through the trees and the windows weren't even open.

Mrs. Ryder paced back and forth at the front of the room. It looked like she'd gotten all the egg stuff out of her dress. She just had a few wet spots on the skirt part.

"I don't know what I was thinking, asking fifth graders to take care of eggs," Mrs. Ryder said. "Obviously I over-estimated you all. I thought you were more mature and responsible than you are."

Alex looked down at her scratched up desktop. She could feel her classmates' dirty looks. She knew they were thinking, *It wasn't us who broke all those eggs. It was Alex.*

Alex wanted to turn around and tell them it wasn't her fault. That she was trying to do the right thing. That was why she came in and got all those eggs in the first place. But it wasn't her turn to talk. It was Mrs. Ryder's.

"I'm curious whether any of you learned anything from this project," Mrs. Ryder began.

Miranda stuck her hand in the air. "I did. I learned—"

Mrs. Ryder cut her off. "Never mind. I don't want to hear what you learned. I want to see it. I'd like each of you to tell me what you learned in a two-page written report."

Several kids groaned.

"Thanks a lot, Alex Hopeless!" Reece muttered.

Alex whirled around. "I am not hopeless!"

"You are, too. If it wasn't for you we'd still be carrying around our eggs and we wouldn't have to do a stupid report."

"I'm not in charge of every single person in this class!" Alex said. "I'm only in charge of myself!" Wasn't that what Mrs. Ryder had said before? That people should take responsibility for their own actions?

But if Mrs. Ryder had noticed that Alex was showing a little responsibility, she sure wasn't saying so. She just said, "Your papers are due this Friday." Then she got out her science book and told everyone to open to page thirty-two.

9

"What happened to your clothes?" Mom asked right away when Alex hopped into the car after school.

Alex told her mom about the fire drill.

Mom sighed. "Unfortunately, we don't have time to stop home so you can change."

"I know," Alex said. Hopefully Dr. Anneling wasn't picky about clean clothes. Alex sniffed the bottom of her shirt. It didn't smell *too* bad.

Mom parked in the hospital parking ramp and they walked inside. Dr. Anneling was waiting right outside the elevator on the fourth floor. The baby floor.

"Hello, Laurie. How are you?" Dr. Anneling was tall with straight brown hair and silver wire-rimmed glasses. She had a gentle voice that made Alex think of wisps of dandelion fluff blowing in a breeze.

"And you must be Alex." Dr. Anneling smiled as she offered Alex her hand. "It's nice to meet you."

"You too." Alex smiled back. She liked this Dr. Anneling lady right away.

"Have you ever been up to the maternity floor?"

Alex shook her head.

"Then let me show you around." Dr. Anneling led Alex and her mom through big double doors that opened to a brightly lit yellow hallway. There were balloons on some of the doors that said "It's a Boy!" or "It's a Girl!" And the whole place smelled of flowers.

There was a lady in one of the rooms who was kind of moaning. The door was mostly shut, but Alex could still hear her. Was she okay? Was someone going to check on her?

Dr. Anneling and Mom strolled on past as though they hadn't even heard the woman. Alex had to hurry to catch up.

Dr. Anneling stopped at the nurse's station and introduced Alex and her mom to some of the nurses who were on duty. They all smiled at Alex and told her it was really nice she wanted to be there to see her baby brother or sister be born.

Then Dr. Anneling led them further down the hallway to a room that had windows all the way around. It was the nursery.

"Oh," Alex breathed as she pressed her nose against the glass and peered inside. There were three babies in there, each in his own little glass bed. One had his little fist all curled up and he was crying. The other two were sleeping. Each one had a little knit pink and blue striped cap on his head. They were all such perfect little people! Perfectly formed with a head and body and arms and legs and fingers and toes.

Next, Dr. Anneling led them to one of the rooms where Mom would have the baby. It didn't even look like a hospital room. It looked like a bedroom. The walls were light blue and there was a flowered bedspread on the bed. The bedspread matched the curtains and the wallpaper border up by the ceiling. There was a love seat and a wood rocker and one of those glass beds for the baby. There was even a TV up high. As Alex stepped further into the room, she saw behind her a bunch of cabinets and a little computer on a cart.

"Come over here, Alex." Dr. Anneling stood over by the bed. "I want to show you how this works." First she demonstrated how the bed went up and down. Then she lifted up the bedspread and showed how the whole bottom part of the mattress slid off and the bed turned into a birthing chair.

"Wow!" Alex said.

Dr. Anneling wheeled the computer cart over to the bed and opened it up. There were monitors and stuff in there that the doctor said would make sure both Mom and the baby were doing okay.

"Why wouldn't they be doing okay?" Alex asked.

"Labor and delivery can be hard for both the mom and the baby," Dr. Anneling explained. She reached into one of the cabinets and pulled out part of a skeleton. It was the bottom part, right above the legs. There was a doll inside that cabinet, too.

"Pretend this doll is a baby," Dr. Anneling said as she stuffed the doll inside the skeleton. Then she eased the doll head first through the opening at the bottom of the skeleton. The doll barely fit through the opening.

"See how a baby is born?" Dr. Anneling smiled.

"Sort of." Except now that Alex thought about it, she realized the opening between a lady's legs wasn't as big as the opening at the bottom of that skeleton. There was skin and stuff down there. So how was a baby supposed to get through?

"In any birth, there's always a chance that Mom or baby will need a little extra help," Dr. Anneling explained. "That's why we have the monitors. To let us know how things are progressing. You'll be able to see how the monitors work in the movie. Should we put that on?"

"Okay," Alex said. She snuggled up next to her mom on the loveseat while Dr. Anneling got the TV and VCR set up.

"I'll come back when the movie is over to see if you have any questions," Dr. Anneling said.

The movie began with a lady talking on the phone. She looked really happy and excited. She was telling somebody that her labor pains had started. But she wasn't at the hospital yet. She was at home.

The lady tipped her head back and laughed. Then she leaned over and started unloading the dishwasher while she talked on the phone. She sure didn't look like she was feeling much pain.

The lady's husband came into the room then. "When was your last contraction?" he asked.

"About ten minutes ago," she replied.

The lady was getting into the car now. Her face was really tight and she didn't look quite so happy anymore.

"Breathe, honey," the man said as he helped her with her seat belt.

In the next scene, the lady was at the hospital. Her eyes were squeezed shut and she was making weird sounds—kind of like a wild animal being tortured.

Alex grabbed her braid. Was this how her mom was going to look when she had the baby?

"Push!" the doctor told her. "Push!"

Alex bit her lip. The lady looked like she was pushing as hard as she could. She grit her teeth and gripped her nightgown in her fists. Sweat poured down her face. Her husband tried to wipe it with a washcloth, but she pushed his hand away.

Alex gulped. She wiped her own sweaty hands on her jeans.

The lady continued to push. Pretty soon you could see the tip of the baby's head coming out between her legs. But as suddenly as it appeared, the head went back inside.

Alex chewed on her braid, her eyes glued to the two lines of blood that were trickling down the lady's leg.

Ew! Yuck!

"Ohhhhhh!" the lady moaned.

Alex's heart pounded. She couldn't breathe. She looked away for a second. Just long enough to catch her breath.

By the time she looked back at the screen, the baby's whole head was out. You could see its face. There were streaks of blood and some weird white stuff all over it. Ugh! Whatever it was, it made Alex's stomach lurch.

"Here come the shoulders," the doctor announced as he pulled and twisted the baby's head. First one shoulder wiggled out. Then the other one. Then the whole baby slid out. A bunch of blood and other stuff squirted out, too.

Alex grabbed her stomach. She wasn't feeling so good.

Alex covered her mouth and ran out of the room.

* * *

"Alex?" Her mom was right behind her. "Alex, what's the matter?"

Alex kept going. If she wasn't careful, she was going to be sick right here in the hallway.

Where was the bathroom?

WHERE WAS THE BATHROOM?

"Is this going to be too much for you, Alex?" Mom asked.

"No!" Alex stopped. Maybe if she just leaned here against the cool wall and took some deep breaths she'd feel better.

Mom smoothed the bangs back from Alex's forehead. "It's okay if it is too much. That's why Dr. Anneling wanted to show you that movie. She wanted you to see what childbirth is really like."

Alex didn't know what she expected childbirth to be like. But what she saw in that movie wasn't it. For one thing, childbirth was painful. Not fall-down-and-scrape-your-knee painful. *Really* painful.

And there was blood and other stuff that was kind of disgusting.

"You look like you could use a drink of water. There's a drinking fountain right over there." Mom squeezed Alex's shoulder and walked over with her.

Alex took a sip of cold water, then let it run over her forehead, cheek and chin. When she finished, she wiped her face in her shirt.

"Better?"

Alex nodded.

"Maybe you want to go over to Ben's house when the baby's born?" Mom asked.

"No!" Alex shook her head. "I still want to be there when the baby's born."

"Are you sure?"

Alex bit her lip. She did want to be there. She just didn't want the birth to be like that movie.

But after all the fuss she'd made about seeing the baby be born, what would people think if she backed out now?

Alex nodded. "I'm sure I want to be there."

10

What if I can't handle it? Alex wondered as Mom drove home from the hospital. *What if I pass out or something?*

"Should we stop and pick up some chicken for dinner on the way home?" Mom asked.

"Sure," Alex said, even though she wasn't very hungry.

"What are you in the mood for? A wonder-roast chicken from the grocery store or KFC?"

"I don't care."

"You choose," Mom said.

But Alex didn't want to choose. She could hardly stand to think about food when her brain was so full of images from that movie.

And Dr. Anneling had said that was a "normal birth." What if Mom didn't have a normal birth? What if something went wrong? What if all those monitors they hooked up to Mom or the baby started beeping? And what if the people in the hospital couldn't figure out what was wrong?

Sometimes babies and even mothers died during childbirth. Alex had seen it on TV.

And as Ben pointed out, Alex wasn't good at emergencies. She freaked out easily. And it was even harder to pay attention and follow directions when she was freaked out.

"Alex?" Mom glanced worriedly at Alex in the rearview mirror. "Are you okay?"

"Huh? Yeah, I'm fine." Alex didn't want her mom to know how badly the movie had shaken her up. That would only prove to everyone that Alex couldn't handle being there when the baby was born.

Think, Alex! What was Mom talking about? Oh, yeah! Food. Chicken. Wonder-roast or KFC?

"I just can't decide what kind of chicken I want tonight," Alex said as she played with the end of her braid.

"Well, how about we go with KFC," Mom suggested.

"Okay," Alex said.

On Thursday, Alex's dad came home. "How's my favorite girl?" he asked as he picked her up and swung her around.

"Fine," Alex said. "Except maybe you shouldn't call me your favorite girl anymore."

"Why not?" Dad asked as he set Alex down.

Alex blinked away the dizziness. "Because what if the baby is a girl? You don't want to play favorites."

"That's true." Dad sat down on the couch and patted the spot next to him. Alex plopped down. "Maybe I should call you my favorite Alexandra Alycia?"

"Okay." Alex grinned.

Dad gave Alex a squeeze. "So," he said, stretching his arms above his head. "How was the hospital visit?"

Alex's grin froze. "It was okay."

"Just okay?" Dad cocked his head at her.

"No, it was good. It was fun. It was interesting." Were those the right words?

"You still think you want to be my assistant labor coach?"

Mom came into the living room from the kitchen then. "Are you guys going to let me?" Alex asked, glancing from her mom to her dad. It wouldn't be backing out if they were the ones who said she couldn't do it.

"Well, Dr. Anneling says it's up to us," Mom said. "Is this still something you think you want to do?"

Alex swallowed hard. "Yes." Sort of.

Mom and Dad exchanged a look.

"I guess we'll give it a try," Mom said.

Alex blinked. They were saying *yes? Were they out of their minds?*

"Grandma's going to come and stay with us before the baby's born, so she'll be at the hospital, too," Mom went on. "If it gets to be too much for you, she can take you out to the waiting room."

"Or she can take you home, if necessary," Dad put in.

"Okay." Alex grabbed her braid.

"It will be nice to have all of us there when the baby is born," Mom said with a smile.

"Yes, it will," Dad agreed.

Alex bit her lip. *What if she couldn't handle it?*

* * *

During recess on Wednesday, Alex played capture the castle with Ben and a bunch of third and fourth graders.

She was guarding the bridge on the climbing structure when Ian and a couple of first graders came along. The first graders weren't playing, so Alex let them cross the bridge.

But when Miranda and Kaila came along, she stood in the middle so they couldn't come up. "What's the password?" she asked. It was the only way she could allow Miranda and Kaila up on the bridge.

"We're not playing," Miranda said as she tucked a piece of hair behind her ear.

Alex had fallen for that one before. She'd let kids

who claimed they weren't playing come up only to have them laugh and yell out, "We won! We captured the castle!"

But Miranda wasn't much for running and chasing games, so maybe she was telling the truth?

Miranda hugged the fire pole and squinted up at Alex in the bright sun. "My mom's a nurse at the hospital," she said out of the blue.

"That's nice," Alex replied. "My mom works at a day care center."

"She said a girl around my age came in yesterday to see the babies and stuff because she was going to be there when her mom had a baby," Miranda went on. "Was that girl you?"

Alex stiffened. "Maybe."

There was only one hospital in town. What were the odds another girl around their age had gone in there yesterday to talk about being there when her mom has a baby?

"So you really are going to be there when your mom has her baby?" Kaila looked really amazed.

Alex shrugged. Her parents had said she could be there, so yeah, it sounded like she would be. Unless she freaked out and Grandma Morgan took her out before the baby was born.

"That's so cool," Miranda said. "Can we come see

the baby after it's born?"

Alex just about fell off the bridge. Miranda and Kaila were the nice girls. The girls who never got in trouble. Not even for talking. And they wanted to come over to Alex's house?

"Um, yeah. I guess so," she said. "If you want to."

"We do," Kaila said.

"Do you want to jump rope with us?" Miranda offered.

"Right now?"

"Well, we need three people to use the big ropes," Kaila said.

Miranda and Kaila had never asked Alex to play before. Never!

"Okay," she said as she hopped off the bridge. "I want to go play with these guys," she told Ben. "Can you find someone else to guard the bridge?"

Ben raised an eyebrow in surprise.

I know! She raised her eyebrow back. She was just as shocked as he was. But she didn't want to let this opportunity slip away.

It was because she was going to be there when the baby was born. People saw her differently now. They didn't see the same old loud and out-of-control Alex. Instead they saw a girl who was mature and responsible. Alex liked being thought of as a girl who was mature and responsible.

The three girls took turns turning the rope and jumping. Miranda and Kaila knew all kinds of jump rope rhymes. And both of them could jump rope way longer than Alex.

Jump! Jump! Jump! They never missed. Their turns jumping seemed to go on forever.

Alex's turn never lasted more than about six seconds. Her braid slapped against her back. Jump! Jump! Miss!

They usually gave her an extra turn, though. Which Alex thought was very nice of them.

Everything was going really well until she caught a glimpse of Reece's blond head out the corner of her eye.

"Got your hat! Got your hat!" Reece laughed as some poor little kid jumped up and down, trying to retrieve the hat that Reece was holding out of reach.

Except that wasn't just any old little kid. It was Ian Munk. Alex's kindergarten buddy.

The rope slipped out of Alex's fingers. "Hey!" She stormed over to the two boys. "Give him back his hat," Alex reached for the hat, but Reece whipped it out of her grasp.

"Are you going to make me?" Reece grinned.

Alex hated that grin. She wanted to take her fist

and knock out every single one of his teeth like dominoes. Bam! Bam! Bam!

But instead she just gave him a shove. "Give it back!"

Reece's grin disappeared. "Don't push me!"

So Alex pushed him again. Harder this time. She actually knocked him back two or three steps. "Then give him back his hat."

By this time, kids were starting to gather around to see what was going on. Ian watched Alex wide-eyed.

Reece glanced at their audience. "You push me again, you'll be sorry," he warned.

"If you don't give Ian back his hat, you'll be sorry," Alex countered. Then she gave him another shove to show she was serious.

"That's it." Reece narrowed his eyes. Then he came at her, butting his head into her stomach, knocking her to the ground.

Before Alex knew it, she and Reece were rolling around on the ground while a bunch of kids stood around them cheering, "Fight! Fight! Fight!"

"Stop it!" Alex yelled. She tried to scramble away from Reece, but Reece grabbed her by the braid and pulled her back to him.

Tears sprang to Alex's eyes. It felt like her braid

was being ripped from her head. She tried to pull free from Reece's grasp, but Reece only pulled tighter.

She kicked and thrashed with both arms and both legs as hard as she could until...Whomp! Her foot rammed into Reece's leg.

Reece swore as he doubled over in pain.

"Serves you right," Alex muttered as she scooted away on her butt. She massaged her aching scalp. Her elbow hurt. So did her knee.

Reece sat up. He glared at her. Then he lunged at her again, knocking her backwards. But before she even hit the ground, Alex felt someone catch her under the arms and pull her out of the way.

Alex turned. It was Mrs. Ryder.

Mr. Cole, one of the fourth grade teachers, grabbed Reece. "Come on. Break it up, you two," he said.

Mrs. Ryder pulled Alex to her feet. "What's going on here?"

Alex's elbow throbbed. There was dirt in her braid and her jeans were torn.

"He was picking on a kindergartener," she explained. She glanced at all the kids who were standing around, figuring someone would speak up and say something like *that's right. He was picking on a kindergartener.* But none of them did. Not even Ben.

"I was just playing," Reece argued. "It was no big

deal. But look what Alex did to my leg!" He tried to roll up his pant leg, but he couldn't get it past his ankle because Mr. Cole had too strong of a hold on him.

"Tell it to Mr. Mallett," Mr. Cole said, nudging Reece toward the school. "Let's go."

Mrs. Ryder had hold of Alex by the back of her jacket. She guided Alex toward the school, too.

Alex gulped. She hadn't been sent to Mr. Mallett's office once this whole school year. She should have known her luck couldn't last.

Mr. Cole yanked open the door with one hand and shoved Reece into the school with the other. Alex and Mrs. Ryder followed behind.

The school was quiet. Too quiet. As they tromped up the stairs to Mr. Mallett's office, Alex felt sick. Her heart pounded harder with every step she took. She felt it in her stomach, her fingers and her throat. Her legs were shaky. Was it possible for a heart to pound so hard that it actually exploded?

Mrs. Paschke, the school secretary, glanced up over her computer as the four of them clattered into the office.

"These two were fighting on the playground," Mr. Cole said.

Mrs. Paschke pinched her lips together, then flipped up the card file on her desk. "I'll call their parents."

Mrs. Ryder led Alex to one wooden bench. Mr. Cole led Reece to the other.

And then they waited for their parents to come.

* * *

"Suspended?" That was Alex's mom. She sounded totally shocked. After all, Alex had never been suspended before.

Alex's dad sounded more like he just wanted to understand. "You mean Alex can't come to school for three days?"

Alex sat wedged between her parents like an Alexandra Hopewell sandwich. One shoulder rested against her mom and the other shoulder rested against her dad.

Reece's mom hadn't come to get him yet, so he was still stuck out in the main part of the office.

"We have a zero-tolerance policy regarding fighting here at Central," Mr. Mallett explained as he made a church steeple out of his fingers. "That means you get into a fight on school property, you're automatically suspended."

"But he was picking on a kindergartener," Alex said.

"That's no excuse for fighting," Mr. Mallett replied.

Alex disagreed. She knew there wasn't supposed

to be any fighting at school. But fifth graders shouldn't pick on kindergarteners, either. If fighting was the only way to make Reece stop, what else was she supposed to do?

"Fighting is never an acceptable way to solve problems," Mr. Mallett went on. "There are always other ways."

"Like what?" Alex asked.

"When you return from your suspension, you and Ms. Westley will be discussing that very matter," Mr. Mallett said as he stood up. "We'll see you back here on Tuesday, Alex. I hope you'll think about what you could have done to prevent this."

And that was it. Mr. Mallett showed them to the door.

A well-dressed woman who smelled like she'd taken a bath in perfume paced angrily back and forth on high heels in front of Reece when Alex and her parents came out of Mr. Mallett's office.

"I hope you're happy!" the woman ranted at Reece. "I had to leave a very important meeting to come down here and pick you up."

Reece just sat there like a lump. It gave Alex a little feeling of satisfaction to see his mom sort of yelling at him.

"I don't know why you couldn't just sit here

outside the principal's office all day," the woman went on. "That would've been fine with me. But no, they said I had to come down and get you."

Then the woman noticed Alex's parents. "Kids, huh?" she said to Alex's mom. "I don't know about you, but I should've gotten a dog instead of a kid. It would be a lot less trouble!"

What a terrible thing for your own mother to say about you, Alex thought.

Reece didn't seem particularly bothered by his mom's comment, though. He raised his chin and said with a smirk, "Yeah, but a dog wouldn't be as interesting as me."

"Watch your mouth!" Reece's mom said. Then they went in to talk to Mr. Mallett and Alex and her parents left.

Alex knew there was going to be trouble when she got home. Her parents would probably just sit her down for ten hours to talk about how disappointed they were in her and remind her she had to get control of herself and learn to make better decisions.

They might ground her, too. They might take away TV or computer time. In fact . . . they might even decide Alex can't be there when the baby is born.

Clearly she wasn't very responsible. Responsible

people did not get suspended. And people who got suspended surely didn't deserve to see their baby brother or sister be born.

Yes! Alex thought. Maybe this was her way out.

11

Everything started out just like Alex expected. Mom and Dad took her home, then sat her down at the kitchen table to talk about what happened.

"Reece was picking on my kindergarten buddy," Alex tried to explain again. "He took Ian's hat and wouldn't give it back. Somebody had to stick up for Ian."

"Couldn't you have told a teacher or done something else besides get into a knockdown drag out fight?" Mom asked.

"Reece knocked me down. He's the one who started fighting." Though Alex had to admit she had pushed first.

"What is it with you and this boy, Reece?" Dad asked. "Why do you two keep having so many problems?"

Alex shrugged. "I don't know." She and Reece had just always had problems. Ever since they were both in speech in first grade.

"It doesn't look like he's got a very good home life,"

Mom said to Dad. "Did you hear his mother? He probably picks on other kids because it makes him feel better about himself."

"Why would picking on other kids make him feel better about himself?" Alex asked.

"Because picking on you makes you feel bad, right?" Mom responded.

Alex nodded.

"Well, when you feel bad, *that* makes him feel *good,*" Mom went on. "He feels big and tough and powerful when he makes you feel bad."

Alex grit her teeth. If that was true, then Reece was just plain mean.

Mom got up then and took a white package out of the freezer and stuck it in the microwave. Dad reached for the mail. Was this conversation over?

Alex cleared her throat. "So, am I going to be punished for getting suspended?"

Her parents glanced at each other. "I think the suspension is your punishment for fighting," Mom said.

"Yeah, I know." Alex twisted her braid around her finger. "But are you going to punish me at home, too? You know, by telling me I can't be there when the baby's born?" Alex's heart pounded.

Her parents exchanged another look. "Do you

think we should do that?" Dad asked.

"I don't know," Alex said carefully. "Do you think you should?"

"I don't think that's necessary," Mom said. "Unless you do?" She raised an eyebrow at Alex.

"No, no, no!" Alex said quickly. Because she knew that was what she was supposed to say. But inside she was thinking *yes, yes, yes!*

On Thursday, Mom went to work, while Alex hung out at home with her dad. It felt weird to watch Ben walk on past her house on his way to school that morning. Alex tapped on the window, but he didn't see her.

"Just because you're home doesn't mean you're on vacation these three days," Dad said. He made Alex keep up with her math and then he made her help paint the baby's room. She didn't mind the painting. That was actually kind of fun.

But on Friday, when she finished her math, Dad made her help clean the garage. First they took everything out and piled it in the driveway. Alex swept the floor and Dad hosed it down. Then they had to find places for all the stuff that was on the driveway. It took a long time. They were still working when Ben walked by after school.

"Hi, Ben!" Alex waved.

Ben waved back, but he kept on walking.

"Can I go play with Ben?" Alex asked her dad.

"When the garage is clean."

Alex frowned. That would take forever. But she knew there was no changing her dad's mind, so she kept working.

By the time Mom pulled into the driveway a couple hours later, they were almost done. "Hey, nice job, you guys," she said when she got out of the car. She looked around like she was in someone else's garage.

"Thanks." Dad gave her a peck on the cheek, then rubbed her large stomach. "How was work?"

Mom closed the car door. "Fine. Except I don't know what we're going to do about Alex on Monday."

"Didn't you ask for the time off?"

"Well, I was going to, but Marcia's on vacation. And now Ann needs the day off, too, because her mom's in the hospital. There really isn't anybody else to take my place."

"You know I fly out again Sunday night," Dad said.

"I know."

"I could stay here alone," Alex said. "I don't mind."

"Not all day, honey," Mom said. She glanced across the street.

Alex followed her gaze. "Olivia's house?" It was one thing to spend a few minutes with Olivia, but the whole day? They ate weird food over there and they didn't have TV and Alex would probably have to do school all day.

"They have some different ideas," Mom admitted. "But they're nice people. It was Mrs. Greene who convinced me it would be okay to have you there when the baby's born."

Alex knew that was supposed to make her feel better, but it actually made her feel worse.

Mom went across the street to talk to Olivia's mom and Alex helped Dad finish putting the rest of the stuff in the garage. Maybe Mrs. Greene would say no. Maybe she'd say Alex was a bad influence and she couldn't have Alex hanging around all day.

No such luck.

Mom came back with a big smile on her face. "It's all set. Alex will spend Monday with the Greene's."

Great, Alex thought. Just great.

* * *

On Saturday, Alex spent the afternoon at Ben's house while her mom and dad attended a childbirth class at the hospital. When she got there, Ben was on the Internet looking at a bunch of other people's football picks.

"Isn't that cheating?" Alex asked.

"No. There's nothing wrong with looking at other people's picks."

"Why'd you pick Green Bay over Minnesota?" Alex asked.

"Minnesota hasn't been doing so hot. And two of our best players are out."

"Still. They're our team. You should pick them as a show of support. Even if you don't think they'll win."

"That's not how you do pick 'ems!" Ben said coolly.

"Okay, okay." Alex went over to the couch and plopped down. Apparently Ben was having a hard time with this week's list. It was best to let him choose his picks in private.

"How long is it going to take you to finish up?" Alex picked up the *TV Guide*.

"I don't know."

Alex tossed the *TV Guide* back down. There was never anything good on on Saturdays.

"Maybe when you're done we can go for a bike ride."

Ben whirled around. "Look, I didn't invite you over today, so I don't have to entertain you."

Alex gaped at her friend. Since when did she need an invitation?

"A-are you mad at me?"

Ben turned back to the computer without answering.

Alex leaped up. "Are you?"

Ben still didn't answer, so Alex spun his chair around and forced him to face her. She gasped when she saw the closed off expression on his face. Ben *was* mad at her.

"Why are you mad at me?" She and Ben hardly ever got mad at each other.

Ben shrugged. He picked at a spot on his jeans. "You're just so weird lately."

"What do you mean?" Olivia Greene was weird. She wasn't.

"I don't know. It's like all you think about is babies and being there when your mom has her baby."

"I'm not thinking about that anymore. In fact, I don't think I want to be there when my mom has the baby. But you can't tell anyone at school. They'll make fun of me after I made such a big deal about it."

"That too!" Ben leaned back against his chair. "You make a big deal about everything. And you get in fights—"

"What are you talking about? I hardly ever get in fights. Except for this thing with Reece, I haven't been in a fight in like two years."

"Yeah, but you used to get in fights all the time."

Alex frowned. "A lot of those fights were with kids who were picking on *you.*"

"I never asked you to fight those kids!" Ben's voice was growing louder. "And neither did Ian."

Alex threw up her hands. "Reece was picking on him! What else was I supposed to do?"

"Let somebody else handle it?" Ben suggested, his voice rising. "Why do you always have to do something? Why can't you ever let things go?"

"I don't know." Alex had never really thought about it. It was just the way she was.

Ben stood up. "Didn't you realize that if you took Reece on, you'd end up in a fight? That you'd get suspended? Didn't you think about that at all?"

"I guess not." At the time, all she thought about was making Reece stop.

"Well, that's the problem. You never think!" Reece threw his hands up in the air. "I'm tired of having a friend who never thinks!" With that, he stomped out of the family room and up the stairs to his bedroom, where he promptly slammed the door.

Alex just stood there trembling. She'd never seen Ben so worked up before. He was usually so cool, calm and collected. She was the one who got all wigged out about things. He was the one who calmed her down.

But not this time.

Alex could handle Mrs. Ryder being mad at her. She could handle having other kids mad at her. But she couldn't handle having Ben mad at her.

Alex could feel the injustice of it all bubbling up inside her like hot lava. She had to get control of herself. Had to get control.

But control was slipping away.

She couldn't take it.

So she put her hands over her ears and SCREAMED!

Ben's mom came running. She said something, but Alex couldn't hear her over her own screaming. "Ben hates me! He hates me!"

Kate grabbed Alex's arms. "Stop screaming, Alex. Stop screaming."

But Alex couldn't stop. Tears poured out of her eyes like running water. Finally Kate took Alex in her arms and held her while she sobbed.

"Shh." Mrs. Casey stroked Alex's head until she calmed down. "It's okay."

Alex cried and cried until she was all cried out. "Ben hates me," she said again with a big sniff.

Mrs. Casey dried Alex's tears with her finger. "No, he doesn't. He's a little upset right now. And I'm not sure he even knows what he's upset about. But when he figures it out, you two will work things out. I'm sure of it."

Alex wished she could be sure, too. Having Ben mad at her was the worst thing that had ever happened to her.

12

Dad dropped his overnight bag on the floor by the front door on Sunday afternoon. He was wearing his airline uniform and cap. "This will be my last overseas trip until after the baby's born," he said, wrapping his arms around Mom.

Mom tipped her head for a kiss. "Good," she said.

"I'll be back in a few days," Dad promised. "Don't have the baby while I'm gone, now."

"I wouldn't dream of it," Mom replied.

"And you help your mother while I'm gone," Dad told Alex.

"I will." Alex wrapped her arms around his neck and squeezed. It was harder saying good-bye to Dad today than usual. It seemed like people were abandoning her left and right. First Ben. Now her dad.

But he had to go. It was his job.

Alex spent the rest of the day moping around the house, wondering if she dared go over to Ben's house. But if she did go over, what would she say?

Everything he said about her was true. She should've known better than to get in a fight with Reece. Even if Reece was picking on Ian. She should've thought about what would happen. But what else could she have done? Let Reece torment Ian?

Now Ben didn't want her around. She couldn't go to school. And she was doomed to spend the next day with Olivia Greene, of all people. Who knew what that would be like?

On Monday morning, Alex grabbed her backpack and trudged down the stairs.

"Don't look so glum." Mom cupped Alex's chin in her hand. "You might actually enjoy yourself over at the Greenes."

"I might," Alex admitted. But she doubted it.

"Now remember. No outbursts over there. You have to be in control of yourself. Mind your manners and do what Mrs. Greene tells you to do." In other words, Ben's mom had seen Alex freak out before, so she could handle it. But Mrs. Greene might not be able to.

"I'll be good," Alex promised on her way out the door. She glanced over her shoulder at Ben's house as she crossed the street, wondering what would happen if they accidentally ran into each other. Would he talk to her?

But it was 8:40. Ben was already at school.

"What good timing," Mrs. Greene opened the door before Alex even knocked. She held Grace in one arm. "I was just going to put Grace down for her nap."

Grace waved her arms excitedly at Alex. Spit dribbled down her chin.

Alex jiggled Grace's hand. "Hi, Grace," she said. Grace was the one good thing about spending the day with the Greenes.

"I see you brought your schoolwork," Mrs. Greene said. "You can go get set up at the kitchen table. Olivia is already in there."

Alex hadn't been inside Olivia's house very often. She was surprised how messy it was. Somehow, she always pictured Olivia's family as really picky-neat. But on her way to the kitchen, she hopped over a gazillion books, blankets and baby toys that were scattered around the living room floor.

"Alex! You're here!" Olivia popped up from her kitchen chair like a jack-in-the-box. She had on a blue flowered dress and ankle socks. Her hair hung in a long braid down her back just like Alex's.

"Isn't it great?" Olivia clapped her hands together. "We get to do school together today."

Alex set her backpack on the table. "Yeah. That's great." At least Olivia didn't hate her.

"Do you want some juice?" There was a tall glass of red juice in front of Olivia. "Or banana bread?"

Alex checked out the plate of banana bread in the middle of the table. It looked like regular banana bread, but knowing the Greenes, it probably had a bunch of weird things in it.

Still, Alex was going to be here all day. She'd have to eat something and the banana bread didn't look too bad. "Okay," she said as she eased herself into a chair.

Olivia slid across the kitchen floor in her stocking feet. She grabbed a glass out of the dishwasher and a pitcher of juice out of the refrigerator and plopped them on the table in front of Alex.

Alex helped herself to a piece of banana bread and poured herself some juice. "Hey, this isn't bad," she said through a mouthful of crumbly bread.

"Are you comfortable, Alex?" Mrs. Greene asked when she breezed into the kitchen a few minutes later.

"Huh?"

"You can't do good work if you're not comfortable. What kind of schoolwork do you have?"

Alex pulled her crumpled worksheets out of her backpack. "I have to do these math worksheets and I have to write a report on ultrasound. I don't know what else." Mrs. Ryder hadn't said what else she'd be missing during her suspension.

Olivia's mom squinted at Alex's worksheet. "Hmm. That's a lot of math."

"Tell me about it," Alex grumbled. And it was all

story problems. Again.

Olivia's math didn't even look like real math. She had all these sticks that she was lining up and putting together in different combinations. "They're Cuisenaire Rods," Olivia explained. She showed Alex how she could use them to do addition, subtraction, multiplication and division.

"Cool," Alex said.

Olivia didn't even have a math book or worksheets. All her math was done with those sticks. Alex wished they had stuff like that at school.

After math, Alex dug out the pamphlets on ultrasound her mom had given her and started her report, while Olivia sat across from her, writing sentences for her spelling words.

Alex rested her head against her hand. She knew she was supposed to read the stuff on ultrasound and then write it in her own words for her report. But she didn't know how to do that. Besides, why should she put it all in her words when the words in the pamphlet were already so good?

Ultrasound can tell you many things about your fetus. For instance . . . , Alex wrote.

After a little while, Olivia said, "Hey, Alex. Do you want see my Egypt stuff?"

"What Egypt stuff?"

"I've been doing a unit study on Egypt. Come on. I'll show you."

Olivia had a ton of stuff to show Alex. She'd drawn a map of Egypt and pictures of Egyptian people in their native clothes. She also had these little blocks of wood. Each one had a little hieroglyph shape that was made out of some foamy stuff and glued onto the piece of wood.

"They're stamps. See?" Olivia opened an inkpad, picked up one of the blocks, plopped it in the ink, then onto a piece of paper. "This is a B."

Alex frowned at the inky figure. "It looks like a foot."

"I know. That's the symbol the ancient Egyptians used for the B sound."

"How do you know all this stuff?" Alex asked. Olivia was only eight, but knew way more than Alex about Egypt.

"I told you. I did a unit study on Egypt. Should we do science now?"

Olivia's "science" turned out to be a study of the ear. She had made a model of the ear with a flour and water paste on cardboard. Now that it was dry, she needed to label all the parts.

Alex wasn't sure how she could help. She didn't know the parts of the ear and what they did. But

Olivia's mom handed her a library book and told her to open up to the big diagram in the middle. For the next half hour, Alex helped Olivia mark the parts on her model and Olivia told Alex what all those parts did.

When Grace got up from her nap, Olivia's mom said they could take a break and play with her. They built block towers for Grace to knock down and played hide the bunny. Babies were so much fun! Alex couldn't wait to have her own baby brother or sister to play with.

"Hey, Olivia," Alex asked as Grace crawled after a bright yellow ball. "What was it like when your mom had Grace?"

Olivia shrugged. "It was okay."

"Was it . . . scary?"

"Well, I got kind of scared when the lady said we might have to go to the hospital."

"The hospital? But I thought your mom and dad don't like hospitals."

"They don't. But they didn't think Grace was ever going to come out. You can die having a baby, you know."

Yes, Alex knew.

"My mom's not crazy," Olivia went on. "She'll go to the hospital if she's going to die."

"B-b-but your mom didn't die."

"No. My dad and the midwife helped her and Grace was born and everything was fine."

Hmm. Alex was beginning to wonder if she should teach at a day care center rather than deliver babies. There was a lot that could go wrong when someone had a baby.

"Girls!" Olivia's mom called. "Lunch is almost ready. Why don't you go out to the garden and get some lettuce and carrots and tomatoes for a salad."

"Okay," Olivia said.

Alex scrambled to her feet and followed Olivia out the back door and over to the huge vegetable garden that took up like half the Greenes backyard. Alex pulled long carrots out of the ground while Olivia cut the lettuce.

By the time they got back inside, Mrs. Greene had set steaming bowls of macaroni and cheese in front of three places at the kitchen table. Macaroni and cheese was actually one of Alex's favorite foods. But she liked Kraft macaroni and cheese. Not only was this stuff not Kraft, it didn't come out of a box at all. Mrs. Greene had made it with twisty noodles and real cheese and baked it in the oven.

Alex peered at the food in front of her. She poked it with her fork. It looked all right. It actually smelled kind of good. So she took a bite.

Not bad. At least Mrs. Greene hadn't served tofu or seaweed. No way would Alex have been able to choke down anything like that.

After lunch, Grace took another nap and Olivia's mom read to Alex and Olivia from a book called *Anne of Green Gables*. Normally Alex didn't like listening to long chapter books. Without pictures, it was hard to follow what was going on in the story. But Olivia's mom said there wasn't going to be a test on the story and not to worry if she missed anything. She even let Alex draw while she listened.

When Olivia's mom finished reading, school was over. And it was only one thirty in the afternoon!

"Don't you have school until three o'clock?" Alex asked.

"Why?" Olivia asked. "We did a lot of work today. Do you want to go outside?"

"You can go outside before three o'clock?"

Olivia and her mom laughed. "School's over," Olivia's mom said. "Go get some fresh air."

So Alex and Olivia went outside. Olivia got out her oversized green ball and they started bouncing it back and forth.

Bounce. Bounce. Bounce.

"Did you like having school at my house today, Alex?"

"I guess so," Alex replied as she bounced the ball back to Olivia. In fact, once she thought about it, Alex realized she liked it a lot.

"Was it different than your school?"

"Oh yeah." Alex nodded hard. "A lot different."

"How?"

"Well," Alex caught the ball and held it against her chest. How could she compare the two? "We have a lot of worksheets and stuff at school. And we have to listen to the teacher talk a lot. We don't get to take a break in the middle to play with our baby sisters. But I guess we do get recess. That's sort of a break."

Alex bounced the ball back to Olivia. "Do you ever wish you went to regular school?" she asked.

Olivia shook her head. "I don't think I'd like it very much."

Alex took one look at Olivia's old-fashioned dress and agreed. "I don't think you would, either. There's a lot more to school than just school work."

"Like what?"

"Well, there's a lot of other stuff you have to worry about. Like whether you're wearing the right clothes or the right shoes. Or whether your hair is okay. Or whether your teacher likes you. Or whether the other kids like you. Sometimes your best friend even stops liking you."

It still hurt Alex to think about her fight with Ben. Would they ever make up?

"Why is it so important what everybody else thinks of you? My mom says it's more important what you think of yourself than what other people think of you."

"That's maybe true when you're homeschooled," Alex said. "But not when you go to school."

When Mom came to pick Alex up a couple hours later, she asked Olivia's mom how everything went.

"Just fine," Mrs. Greene replied. "No trouble at all. Alex was a joy to have around."

Alex stared at Mrs. Greene. No one had ever said anything like that about her before.

13

"I think I should quit school and have you homeschool me," Alex announced when she and her mom got home.

"Excuse me?" Mom glanced over at Alex as she rifled through the mail.

Alex dropped her backpack on the table. "I wouldn't get in so much trouble if I was homeschooled. You heard Mrs. Greene. She said I was a joy to have around."

Mom smiled. "You are a joy to have around. But I don't think homeschooling is a good idea. It works for the Greenes, but I'm not so sure it would work for us."

"Why not?"

"Well, first of all, I have a job."

"You'll have time off when the baby's born," Alex pointed out.

"Only eight weeks. What would we do when I go back to work?"

"I could go with you. I could use those math sticks that Olivia has and I could make hieroglyphs at the day care center and when I finished, I could help with the babies."

Mom sat down at the kitchen table and motioned

for Alex to do the same. "What's the matter, Alex? Are you nervous about going back to school tomorrow?"

"Sort of." Alex rested one foot over the opposite knee and picked at the loose rubber on her tennis shoe. She couldn't go back to school as long as she and Ben were fighting. She just couldn't.

"You need to face your problems head on, honey. You need to take responsibility for your actions."

"I know." And she was willing to do that. "It's just..."

"Just what?" Mom leaned closer to Alex.

Alex swallowed hard. "It's just I haven't been in a fight in like two years. What if I start getting in more fights?" she asked in a low voice.

"Are you planning on getting into more fights?"

Alex shrugged. Getting into fights wasn't something Alex ever planned on. It just happened.

And it wasn't just the possibility of getting into more fights that worried Alex. She had a teacher who didn't like her, a teacher who didn't understand her. She had no real friends at school, not even Ben. Plus she didn't always understand what she was supposed to do at school. And it always took her longer to do her work than it took anyone else. It just would be better all around if she were homeschooled.

"You know, Alex, when you were having so many

problems in school a few years ago, I considered quitting my job and homeschooling you."

"You did?" Alex perked up. "Why didn't you do it?"

"Well, for one thing, you didn't want me to. You wanted to go to school like everybody else."

Alex didn't remember ever talking about homeschooling before.

"And I thought it was good for you to be around lots of different people. Different kids. Different teachers. It's good for me to be around different people every day, so I thought it would be good for you, too. For the most part, I think it has been good. You've come a long way since first grade."

At the moment, Alex didn't feel like she'd come very far at all.

Mom took Alex's hand. "I want you to go back to school tomorrow, and I want you to try your best to get along with everyone. I want you to try your best to be in control of yourself. Okay?"

Alex didn't say anything.

"Come on, Alex. You're not a quitter."

"Who says I'm not?" Alex grumbled.

Mom sat back against her chair. "Well," she said. "I guess that's up to you. You're the one who decides what kind of person you are. Not me. Not Mrs. Ryder. You! So, if you decide you're a quitter, then I guess you're a quitter."

Alex twirled her braid through her fingers. She couldn't even look at her mom. She hated the look of disappointment in her eyes.

"But if you decide you're a pretty okay kid, the kind of kid who never gives up, the kind of kid who learns from her mistakes, well, then that's the kind of kid you really are," Mom went on.

Alex disagreed. "Everybody thinks I'm some kind of maniac. Even Ben."

"Don't worry so much about what everyone else thinks," Mom said. "You and Ben aren't going to stay mad at each other forever. In fact, I bet if you go over there right now, the two of you will make up."

"I don't know." Alex slid a little lower in her chair. "What would I say?"

Mom rested her hand against Alex's cheek. "Just say whatever's in your heart. Did it ever occur to you that maybe Ben is just as lost without you as you are without him?"

"No." No way. Ben was smart and funny and he knew a lot about sports. Everyone liked Ben. What did he need her for?

But . . . what if he *did* miss her?

"Okay." Alex hopped to her feet. "I'll go over there." She had a feeling Ben would never come to her.

She marched up the Casey's front steps and stabbed at their doorbell.

Ben's mom came to the door.

Alex's heart pounded. She felt like she didn't belong here. But she was already here. She couldn't turn around and go back home now. "I-is Ben here?" she stammered.

Mrs. Casey actually smiled at Alex as she held the door open. "He's up in his room. Why don't you go on up, Alex." She acted like it was just any old day where she and Ben were best friends.

"Okay." Alex's feet were like lead. It was a major effort to pick up each foot and set it down on the next step. Pick it up. Set it down. Pick it up. Set it down. Eventually she reached the top of the stairs.

Ben's room was the first one on the right. Alex stopped in front of the closed door. She knocked— three quick taps, then waited.

"Come in."

Alex slowly opened the door. Ben was leaning against a stack of pillows, reading on the floor. He looked up when Alex shuffled into the room but his face showed no emotion. Was Ben happy to see her or did he wish she'd go away? Alex wondered.

Just say what's in your heart. That was what Mom told her to do. Alex took a deep breath, then said,

"I don't like it when you're mad at me."

"I don't like it when I'm mad at you either."

"Do you think you could stop?"

"Maybe."

Alex sat down on the floor next to Ben and hugged her knees to her chest. They both faced the wall instead of each other.

Alex sighed. "Why are you so mad?" she tried again.

"It's hard to explain. I don't like it when you get in fights. This one especially reminded me how it felt when you beat up kids who were mean to me."

Alex frowned. "How did it feel?"

"Well, part of it felt good because it meant I wasn't completely alone. There was at least one person who liked me."

Alex understood that. She felt that way about Ben, too.

Ben went on. "But it felt bad that I needed you to defend me. That I needed a girl to defend me. That I couldn't defend myself."

"I never minded defending you."

"I know. But I minded. It made me feel bad. Especially when you got in trouble."

Alex never meant for Ben to feel bad.

"Okay, I get that." Alex said. "But I still think it was different with Ian. He's like five years younger than we are. Reece shouldn't have been picking on him and someone needed to stop him."

"Yeah, maybe," Ben gave in. "I'm just saying it reminded me of me at that age. And I didn't like it."

"Okay, if someone tries to beat you up, I promise I won't stop them. Will that make you feel better?"

Ben let out a short laugh. "No one's really tried to beat me up in like three years."

"That's because you've been taking tae kwon do." People would be stupid to take on somebody who knows tae kwon do. Alex's forehead wrinkled. "Is that why you started doing tae kwon do? So you could defend yourself?"

"Partly. But tae kwon do also gave me something in common with the other kids. I was really different from everyone else."

Alex nodded. She remembered.

"I didn't know how to do anything except read. You're the one who taught me how to roller blade and how to play kickball and how to make baskets."

Alex remembered all of that, too.

"You helped me get along better with other kids," Ben went on.

"I did?" Alex was stunned. How could she have helped someone get along better with other kids? She could barely get along with other kids herself.

"Well, doing football picks helped, too. I was never good at playing football. Probably because I'm a year younger than everyone else. Even for a nine-year-old, I'm small."

Alex often forgot that Ben was a year younger than she was. He always acted older.

"But I learned a lot about football by doing picks every week. And then I had something I could talk about with the other guys. Do you know how hard it is to be a guy who doesn't play football?"

Alex had never thought about it. "Maybe I should tell Ian to take up football, huh?"

"Or at least football picks," Ben said.

14

Life at school had gone on without Alex during the three days she'd been gone. First of all, the desks had been rearranged into groups of four instead of the straight rows Alex was used to. Alex's desk was still up front. Right next to Drew and right across from Stafford and Miranda. At least she wasn't by Reece anymore.

The second thing that was different was Miranda had gotten a haircut. Gone were her long beautiful curls. Now her perfect blond hair was cropped close to her face. Alex thought Miranda looked better with long hair, but she was polite enough not to say so.

The third thing that was different was there were boxes with batteries and wires lined up on the counter under a poster that read: *What is Electricity?* Apparently the class had started a unit on electricity. Hopefully that would go better for Alex than the family life unit had.

Which reminded Alex — the family life unit had ended last week. Everyone else had turned in their reports. So she opened her bag and rifled through all the old papers in there until she found her report on ultrasound. She took it up to Mrs. Ryder, wondering if she was going to get yelled at for turning it in late. But Mrs. Ryder just said in her regular voice, "Well! I'm glad to see you did some school work while you were gone, Alexandra."

"I did my math, too." Alex dug through her bag some more, searching for her math folder. There it was. She pulled it out. "Here's Thursday's, Friday's and yesterday's assignments."

Mrs. Ryder took the papers from Alex, then laid them down on her desk. "You know, you and Reece were supposed to meet with Ms. Westley this morning before you came back to class. Reece is already down there. They're probably waiting for you."

"Oh, yeah." Alex had forgotten about that. She and Reece were supposed to talk about what happened last week and how they could have done things differently. Alex still wasn't convinced she should've done things differently. What was she supposed to do? Lie to Ms. Westley?

Alex set her bag on her seat, then tromped down the hall to Ms. Westley's office. Reece was slouched in the bench outside her closed door. He sat up a little when Alex came into the outside office.

"Hey, it's my good friend, Alex Hopeless," he said.

Alex plopped down on the bench as far away from

Reece as she could get. "I am not hopeless," she said "You are too."

"I am not. I decide who I am, not you."

Before Reece could open his mouth to argue, Ms. Westley's door opened and she poked her head out. "You two can come in now."

Alex was closest to Ms. Westley's office, so she went in first. "Hey, you got a plant in here," she noticed right away.

"Yes." Ms. Westley smiled.

Alex used to tell Ms. Westley she needed a plant because her little yellow office was so plain. There was a poster that listed ten keys to success taped to the wall across from the door. But that was the only non-school thing in the whole room, except for the small plant with long pointy leaves that now sat on the edge of her desk.

"Why don't you two sit down," Mrs. Westley gestured toward the two straight-backed chairs in front of her small wooden desk.

Reece slumped into the closest chair. Alex moved the other chair a few inches away from Reece's, then sat down.

Ms. Westley folded her hands across her desk. "Let's talk about what happened last Wednesday, shall we?"

The next few minutes were spent rehashing everything Mr. Mallett had said last week: how the school has a zero tolerance policy for fighting, how there are always better ways to solve problems and so on.

"I don't know what else I could have done," Alex told Ms. Westley. "Fifth graders shouldn't pick on kindergarteners. I was just trying to make Reece stop."

"I wasn't picking on the kid, we were just playing a game," Reece argued, rolling his eyes.

"I don't think Ian was enjoying your game very much."

"How do you know? Did you ask him?"

Ms. Westley cleared her throat. "Actually, I spoke to Ian and a couple of other kindergarteners. They said you took Ian's hat, Reece, and that Alex tried to get it back. Then the two of you got in a fight."

"That's exactly what I said happened!" Alex slapped the desktop with her hand. Finally, someone cared about her side of the story.

Reece smirked. "Hey, I didn't think that kid ever talked."

"He talks," Alex said. "He just doesn't talk to you."

"Reece, I think you took Ian's cap because you knew it would provoke somebody," Ms. Westley said.

"The question is who were you trying to provoke? Ian or Alex?"

The corners of Reece's mouth turned up just a bit, like he was trying to keep himself from smiling.

"I don't see what's so funny," Ms. Westley said in a voice that made the smile on Reece's face disappear.

"Reece is always trying to provoke me," Alex added.

Ms. Westley turned to Alex. "And you're always responding. Why is that?"

Alex felt stung. That wasn't the answer she was expecting. Not from Ms. Westley.

"If Reece would quit—"

Ms. Westley put up her finger to stop Alex. "Reece and I are going to work on his behavior. He's going to stop provoking you."

Hmph, Alex though. Was it even possible for him to stop provoking her?

"And you and I are going to work on your responses to things," Ms. Westley went on. "You don't need to get so worked up all the time."

Alex couldn't help getting worked up. That was just the kind of person she was.

But maybe she could change? With Ms. Westley's help?

After that Ms. Westley sent them back to their

class. At first, Alex tried to walk a few steps behind Reece, but there was something she wanted to ask him. "Hey, Reece," she said when she caught up to him. "Why do you pick on me all the time?"

Reece let out a short laugh. "Because it's so easy."

"Then you really must feel pretty bad about yourself," Alex said. "Otherwise you wouldn't pick on kindergarteners and people who are easy to pick on."

Reece just stared at her. He didn't seem to know what to say to that.

"I'm going to learn how not to respond to you. But I bet you'll never learn how not to provoke me. I guess that means you're the one who's hopeless, not me!"

With a quick toss of her braid, Alex strolled into their classroom. She'd made up with Ben. She'd put Reece in his place. If only she could figure out how to deal with Mrs. Ryder.

At the end of the day, Mrs. Ryder handed Alex her ultrasound report. There was a bright red D at the top of the page.

"You just copied this out of a book, Alexandra," Mrs. Ryder said. "You didn't use your own words."

"The book I was reading was really complicated and hard to understand," she tried to explain. "I changed the sentences around. I did the best I could."

"Sometimes, Alexandra, your best just isn't good

enough," Mrs. Ryder said. "Maybe your paper on what you learned from this unit will be better."

"You mean I still have to do that? The ultrasound paper wasn't enough?"

"The ultrasound paper was to make up for all the broken eggs. The other paper is to show me what you've learned." Mrs. Ryder continued down the aisle, returning papers.

Alex had tried to do a good job on that paper. Really, she had. But it seemed like no matter what she did, it was never good enough for Mrs. Ryder. And it probably never would be.

"You just don't like me, do you, Mrs. Ryder?" she said in a low voice.

Mrs. Ryder whirled around. Alex could see the look of surprise in Mrs. Ryder's eyes. Mrs. Ryder opened her mouth, then closed it, then opened it again. "What in the world would make you say such a thing?"

Alex shrugged. She stared down at her desk. "I know you don't. I can just tell."

Silence.

Alex suddenly remembered that she and Mrs. Ryder were not alone. The whole class was there, staring wide-eyed at the two of them. Alex slid down in her chair. She had created a scene. Again.

"Class, take out your library books and read for a few minutes," Mrs. Ryder said calmly. "Alexandra, I'd like to speak with you out in the hall."

Alex's heart pounded.

Desks creaked open then banged closed all around the room. Nobody said a word.

Alex rose slowly from her seat and followed Mrs. Ryder out into the hall. Why, oh why, couldn't she ever keep her big mouth shut?

Mrs. Ryder closed the door, then motioned for Alex to go stand by the wall.

Alex stared at the floor. There was a little pile of dirt behind the door stop.

"You and I have a problem, don't we?" Mrs. Ryder said.

Alex raised her eyes briefly, then lowered them again.

"I am hard on you," Mrs. Ryder admitted. "But you try my patience, Alexandra. You try my patience more than any other student I've ever had. I just don't know how to get through to you."

Alex didn't know what she was supposed to say to that.

"Nine times out of ten, I look over at you and you're doing something you shouldn't be doing. If I don't let you know when you're doing the wrong thing, how are you ever going to learn to do the right thing?"

Alex chewed her bottom lip and kept her eyes peeled on that pile of dirt.

"If there's a better way to teach you to do the right thing, by all means, let me know," Mrs. Ryder said.

"Do I ever do the right thing?" Alex asked in a small voice.

"I beg your pardon?"

"I try to do the right thing. Really, I do. But if I ever do do the right thing, you never tell me. You only tell me when I make mistakes. So," Alex shrugged. "I was just wondering whether I ever do the right thing."

Silence.

Uh oh. Had Alex said the wrong thing again?

The bell rang and kids came pouring out of the other classrooms. Alex could see some of the kids in Mrs. Ryder's class peering at her through the window. Nobody dared leave without Mrs. Ryder's permission. But Mrs. Ryder just stood there. Hadn't she heard the bell?

"Um, Mrs. Ryder?" Alex said.

Mrs. Ryder blinked. "Oh! It's time to go." She turned and opened the classroom door. "Come on, class. You know the buses won't wait." Then she turned back to Alex like she wanted to say something, but all she said was, "I'll see you tomorrow, Alexandra."

When Alex got home after school, she was surprised to find her mom's car parked in the driveway. Wasn't Mom supposed to be at work?

Alex tore up the steps to her house and banged open the door. "Mom?" she called.

No answer.

"Mom?" Alex made her way through the living room, dining room and kitchen. The only sign of her mother was the purse she had left on the kitchen table.

Alex headed downstairs to the family room. The lights were turned down low and there was soft violin music playing on the stereo. Mom was lying on the couch with her feet propped up on a stack of pillows. She was breathing really slow.

"Oh, my gosh! You're not having the baby now, are you?" Alex cried. It was too early. Plus Dad wasn't home.

"What?" Mom's eyes flew open. For a moment she looked as panicked as Alex felt. Then her face relaxed. "No, no, no," she said. "The kids really wore me out today, so I came home a little early. I am practicing my breathing exercises, though. Would you like to help?" Mom held out her hand to Alex.

Alex shrugged. "What do I have to do?" she asked as she slowly sat down beside her mother.

"Just breathe with me. We start with slow, deep breathing during early labor. Like this."

Alex watched as Mom took a deep breath in through her nose and slowly let it out through her mouth.

In through the nose and out through the mouth.

There was a certain rhythm to it. A rhythm that matched the violin music exactly. In, two, three, four. Out, two, three, four.

Alex breathed along with her mother.

In, two, three, four.

Out, two, three, four.

Alex closed her eyes and let her body fall back against the couch.

In, two, three, four.

Out, two, three, four.

Over and over.

Alex could feel her whole body relaxing as she breathed in rhythm with the music. The D on her report . . . Reece . . . Mrs. Ryder...all her problems just drifted away as her chest rose and fell with each breath.

Then the music stopped.

Alex opened one eye. Her body felt like dead weight. "You could fall asleep doing this," she said as she opened the other eye and raised herself up onto her elbows.

Mom smiled. She grabbed the remote control off the coffee table and started the music again. "It is relaxing," she agreed. "But whenever I relax, the baby wakes up. He or she is kicking up a storm right now."

"Really?"

"Would you like to feel?"

"Yeah," Alex said, resting her hand lightly on her mother's stomach.

Mom moved Alex's hand up a little higher. "Oh!" Alex felt something press against her hand. "Was that it?"

Mom nodded.

"What does it feel like?"

Mom took a deep breath. "It's hard to explain, Alex. But I can tell you this. Knowing there's life inside me is the most wonderful feeling in the world."

"I bet you wish the baby could just stay inside you forever and you wouldn't ever have to have it." After watching that movie, Alex thought it was amazing anyone had babies.

Mom laughed. "No, I'm getting so big and bulky, I'd just as soon have this baby any time now."

"But it's going to *hurt* when you do."

"Yes," Mom agreed. "But, that's why I'm practicing these different breathing techniques. So I'll be able to handle each stage of pain as it comes. The one we just did should get me through the early stage of labor when the contractions aren't so bad."

"What will you do when the contractions get worse?" Alex wanted to know.

"I'll switch to a more shallow breathing style. Like this."

Mom rubbed her hands together, then laid her hands in her lap. Again, she took a breath in through her nose and let it out through her mouth. But this time the breaths came much faster. Probably twice as fast as the slow breathing.

Watching her mom breathe so fast made Alex feel tired. "How is breathing that fast going to feel better?" she asked.

"Because the faster breathing will give me something else to concentrate on besides the pain."

"What will you do when the contractions are really, really bad?" Alex asked.

"Pant. Like this. He-he-he-he-he-he-he-he-he."

Alex giggled. "You look funny when you do that."

"Well, let's see how you look when you do it!" Mom teased.

"Okay. He-he-he-he-he!" Alex panted.

"That's very good," Mom said.

"He-he-he-he-he!" they panted together. Then they both started laughing.

Once they got control of themselves, Mom looked at Alex. "Honey, how do you really feel about being there when the baby is born? Are you sure this is something you want to do?"

Alex grabbed her braid. "I don't know," she admitted. "I want to be there, but I'm scared. I don't want to see you in so much pain."

Mom took a deep breath. "What if you and Grandma come to the hospital with me and Dad? You can be there in the room to start with. But then when things start to move along, you can go out to the waiting room with Grandma. As soon as the baby's born, you can come back. That way you'll get to see him or her right away. But you won't have to be there for any of the really hard part."

Alex bit her lip. "Do you think I'd be giving up if I did that? You know, after I made such a big deal about wanting to be there?"

"I think what's really important here is do *you* think you're giving up?"

Alex thought about it. "I don't think so."

Mom squeezed Alex's shoulders. "I don't think so,

either. I think you're doing the mature and responsible thing."

"Really?" How was that?

"Everybody has limitations. It takes maturity and responsibility to recognize those limitations," Mom said.

So . . . Mom was saying Alex was mature and responsible after all? Wow. Alex wasn't used to thinking of herself that way. But she could get used to it. She could used to it awfully fast.

15

"What do you say we pick up a pizza and a couple of movies and just relax this evening?" Mom suggested a little later.

Mom even let Alex pick the movies. She chose two scary ones. At least, she hoped they'd be scary. Mom never let her watch anything that was even rated PG-13, which didn't leave many choices.

While the previews for the first movie were on, Mom said, "It won't be long before the baby comes. I'm due in three weeks."

Alex popped a piece of pepperoni into her mouth. "I know. I can hardly wait."

Mom smiled. "I'm glad. I know you've wanted a brother or sister for a long time. But aren't you worried about what it's going to be like around here once you actually have one?"

"No." Alex shook her head. "Should I be?"

"I don't know," Mom replied. "Most kids feel a little uh, displaced when a new baby comes along."

"Displaced?" What did that mean?

"Jealous."

"Oh." Alex took a bite of her pizza. "Why

should I be jealous?"

"Well, babies take a lot of time."

"I know! Mom, I'm not five years old. I don't need your attention all the time."

Mom sighed. "No, I guess you don't. But promise me if you ever feel sad or left out, you'll talk to your dad or me about it."

"I will!" Alex said impatiently. "Now, can we watch the movie?"

"Okay."

They watched the first movie and then Mom put in the second. Somewhere in there Alex must have fallen asleep. When she woke up, the living room was dark.

She thought she heard someone calling her name. She sat up and listened. *No, I must be imagining things,* she decided. *It's the middle of the night.* She thought about going up to bed, but she was too tired to actually get up and go to her room. So she just pulled the afghan up to her chin and lay back down where she was.

Then she heard her name again. Louder this time. "Alex!"

Alex sat up. She rubbed her eyes. She could see a light under the bathroom door at the top of the stairs. She reached over and turned on the table lamp.

"ALEX!!!!!!"

"Mom?" Alex kicked the afghan to the floor and tiptoed up the stairs. She paused outside the bathroom door. "Mom, are you in there?"

"Ohhhhhhhh!" was her mother's response.

Alex turned the knob and opened the door. Her mom was on the floor next to the toilet. Her underwear was on the floor beside her. "Baby!" she said breathlessly.

Alex's jaw dropped. "You're having the baby now?"

Mom nodded. Then she clutched her stomach. "AAAAHHHHH!" she screamed, doubling over.

Alex could feel panic rising in her chest. She didn't know what to do. But she had to do *something*.

"Come on, Mom! Breathe!" Alex cried, dropping to her knees. "Breathe like we did earlier. When you had the music on."

But her mom was ignoring her. She was ignoring her and *not* breathing.

Oh God! Alex thought, grabbing her head. WHAT DO I DO?

Make her breathe!

Alex got right in her mom's face, puffed out her cheeks and took hard, deep breaths. "He-he-he-he-he!"

Mom shook her head. "Too late!" she said, pushing Alex away. "Baby coming!"

Mom shifted position and Alex could see between her mom's legs. There was a big bulge. Like a balloon.

And hair. Dark hair.

Coming out of her mother.

Mom couldn't very well drive to the hospital like that. And there was no one else to drive her, either. *What are we going to do?* Alex screamed inside her head.

"Call Kate!" Mom ordered.

Alex ran to her mother's room and grabbed the cordless phone. She started pushing buttons on her way back to the bathroom.

"Gotta push!" Mom said as she got up into a squatting position.

"NO!" Alex cried. "You can't push. The baby might come out!"

Alex watched as her mom grit her teeth. Beads of sweat bubbled on her forehead. The bulge between Mom's legs was getting bigger. Just like in that movie at the hospital.

Alex pressed the button on the phone. "I'm not going to call Kate," she said. "I'm calling 9-1-1!"

She'd never called 9-1-1 before. She could remember goofing around with Ben once and wanting to call 9-1-1 just to see what happened. But Ben said you should never call 911 unless it was a real emergency.

Otherwise they might not come when you really want them to.

Alex glanced at her mother again. If this wasn't a real emergency, she didn't know what was. She pressed 9, 1, 1.

"Medford Emergency."

"Hello?" Alex's heart was pounding. Her hands were shaking. But she knew this was the right thing to do. "My mom's having a baby," she squeaked.

"Right now?" a man asked.

"Yes."

"The baby's coming out?"

"YES!" Hadn't she just said that?

"Okay, let me transfer you to area ambulance."

"They're not going to get here in time," Mom moaned as she sank back against the vanity.

"Area Ambulance," a woman's voice came on the line.

"Yeah, we need an ambulance," Alex said. "Quick!"

"What is the emergency?"

"MY MOM'S HAVING A BABY! She's having a baby right now!"

"Okay, calm down. Take a deep breath. What's your name, honey?"

"Alex."

"Alice?"

"No. ALEX! Alex Hopewell! I live at 2023 38th St."

"Are they coming?" Mom asked.

There was even *more* head showing now.

"YOU'VE GOT TO HURRY!" Alex screamed into the phone.

"The ambulance is on its way, Alex. But you've got to stay calm. Is there anyone else there with you?"

"No. Just me and my mom."

"And the baby's coming? You can see the head?"

"Yes. It's got dark hair. And it's coming out! Please hurry!" Alex cried. She'd never been so scared in her entire life.

"Okay, Alex. I want you to put your hand flat against the baby's head."

"You want me to push it back in?"

"No! Just gentle pressure. We don't want the head to pop out and tear your mother."

"Okay," Alex whimpered. She rested the phone between her ear and her shoulder. She got down on her knees and reached out to touch the baby's head. It felt hard. Like a rock. But slimy. And the hair didn't even feel like real hair.

"It's popping out anyway!" Alex cried. She could feel it pushing against her hand. "When's the ambulance going to get here?"

"Soon. Real soon."

Mom groaned again and Alex felt more

pressure against her hand.

"THE WHOLE THING'S COMING OUT!" Alex screamed.

"OOOOHHHHHH!!!" Mom moaned. Her whole body twisted in pain.

"Did you say the head is coming out?" the person on the phone asked.

"YES!" Alex exclaimed.

"OH!" Mom cried. "Oh! Oh! Oh! Oh!"

Alex felt her whole insides tingle and she watched the baby's head slide further and further. It was coming out. The whole thing was coming out.

"OOOOOHHHHHH!" Mom screamed. And then, with a pop, the head was out.

"The head's out!" Alex yelled into the phone. She could hardly believe her eyes.

"Is it facing up or down?" the voice on the phone asked..

"Down." All Alex could see was the back of the baby's head.

"Good. That's good. Do you have some towels near by?"

"Towels?" Alex looked around. She and Mom were in the bathroom. There were towels hanging next to the tub. "Yeah. I've got towels."

"Good. I want you to wipe the baby's mouth and nose with a dry towel."

"Okay." Alex's hands shook as she reached down to

wipe the baby's face. She couldn't really see what she was wiping.

"Did you do it?" the voice on the phone asked.

"Here it comes again!" Mom cried, gritting her teeth. "GRRRRRRR!" She sounded like some kind of monster. Not like her mother at all. It was worse than the lady in that movie at the hospital.

"I think more of the baby is coming out!" Alex said.

"Okay, Alex. That's all right. I want you to take the towel and support the baby's head and shoulders as they come out."

"Me?"

"Yes you."

"But when is the ambulance going to get here?"

"Soon. Very soon. Are you holding onto the baby's head? It's going to be very slippery when it comes out."

"Yes," Alex said. "I've got the head." The baby was starting to turn to the side now. Like it heard Alex's voice and wanted to see her.

"Oh, wow," Alex breathed as she saw the baby's face for the first time. It was all red and blotchy, but still, it was a real baby. This was an actual person coming out of her mother.

"Hey, what's that white thing around its neck?" Alex asked.

"White thing?" Mom panted. She leaned forward, straining to see.

"There's something around the baby's neck?" the voice on the phone asked. "The umbilical cord?"

"YES!" Alex screamed, realizing what it was. "It's around the baby's neck! What do I do? What do I do?"

"THE CORD IS AROUND THE BABY'S NECK?" Mom cried.

"Is it wrapped around just once or more than once?"

"Um, I don't know," Alex said, looking down at it. "I think just once."

"Okay, Alex. Listen to me. You've got to move the cord."

Alex gasped. "I can't!"

"Yes, you can!"

Alex shook her head. Her whole body trembled. "No, I can't."

"Alex, calm down. Take a deep breath. You can do this. All you have to do is slide your finger under the cord and carefully pull it over the baby's head."

"Cord?" Mom panted. "Cord around baby's neck?"

"Come on, Alex," the voice on the phone urged. "You can do it."

Alex took a deep breath. She reached for the umbilical cord. It felt smooth and slippery. She slipped her finger underneath it and gave a gentle tug. "It's not moving," she said. Her eyes swelled with tears.

"Keep trying."

Alex's heart was pounding so hard she thought it was going to burst right out of her chest.

"OOOOOOOHHHHHHHH!" Mom moaned. Her knee conked Alex on the head, but Alex hardly noticed.

The baby's going to die! she thought with alarm. *Mom's going to die! Everyone's going to die and*—Oh! With a little more force, the cord stretched. Alex quickly slipped it over the baby's head. "Hey, I did it!" she cried as a small laugh escaped her.

"That's good. Very good," said the voice on the phone.

Alex grabbed her mom's arm. "I got the cord off," she said. But it didn't look like Mom even heard her. Her teeth were clenched. Sweat dripped down her cheeks.

"OOOOOHHHHHHH!" Mom groaned as she pushed even harder.

"You're still holding on to the baby's head?" the voice on the phone asked.

Alex grabbed the towel and quickly placed both hands back under the baby. "Uh huh," she said. She was getting a cramp in her neck from holding the phone with her shoulder. But she didn't dare set the phone down.

"The shoulders are coming now," Alex said.

"Okay. You're doing fine, honey. Just make sure you support the head and the shoulders as they come."

"I am." Alex bit her lip. She held her hands firmly under the baby's head as it slowly made its way out. First one shoulder, then the other.

This was the scariest thing Alex had ever seen. But it was also the most amazing.

Mom leaned back against the bathroom wall. "Oh God!" she moaned, gasping for breath.

"What's happening?" asked the voice on the phone.

"The shoulders—" Alex began. But she was interrupted by a sudden burst of water from between her mother's legs. It splashed onto the floor and onto Alex. Then the whole baby slid into her hands. "Whoa!" Alex said, shifting her balance. The phone slipped off her shoulder and banged to the floor.

"Hello? Hello? Alex? Are you there?"

Mom collapsed against the bathroom wall and burst into tears. Alex felt as though the floor had gone out beneath her. But she couldn't comfort her mother with a baby in her arms. The baby! Alex suddenly realized. IT WASN'T CRYING.

"ALEX!" screamed the phone.

She picked up a corner of the towel and wiped the baby's face with it. Then she grabbed the phone. "The baby's not—"

But then the baby let out an ear piercing cry and Alex breathed a sigh of relief. She nudged her mother, holding the baby in her arms. "Look, Mom!" she cried. The phone clunked to the floor again. "The baby's okay."

"Let me have the baby," Mom sobbed.

Alex carefully placed the baby in her mother's outstretched arms.

"Now you come here, too." Mom sniffed as she held the crying baby in one arm and reached out toward Alex with the other. Alex allowed herself to be pulled into her mother's lap.

"You did it, honey," Mom whispered as she kissed Alex's forehead.

Wow, she thought with amazement. I DID!

"Alex!" the phone barked. "Is everyone okay?"

There was pounding on the door downstairs. "Paramedics," came a man's voice.

Alex got up and hurried down the stairs. Two guys in dark coats were coming in.

"Sure, *now* you guys get here," Alex muttered.

They could hear the baby's screams. "Sounds good and healthy," one of the men said, smiling at Alex.

"So what is it?" the other one said. "A boy or a girl?"

Alex gasped. She hadn't had a chance to find out yet.

16

"I thought it was heartburn," Mom told the paramedics as they transferred her to a low cot. "We had pizza for dinner and . . . " Mom's voice trailed off.

"You did a great job, kid," one of the paramedics told Alex. "This little boy looks healthy as an ox."

"He sure does," agreed the other guy as he wrapped a blanket around the baby. The umbilical cord and placenta kept getting in the way.

"Why don't we just cut that cord here," the first guy said. "We don't need to wait until we get to the hospital."

"Okay," the other guy agreed. He pulled out a plain old pair of scissors and handed it to Alex. "Would you like to do the honors?"

Alex gasped. "Me?"

"Go ahead, Alex," Mom said.

One of the men had put some sort of clamp on the umbilical cord. He showed her exactly where to snip.

Alex took a deep breath. "Okay," she said, closing down on the scissors. To her surprise, the scissors cut easily through the cord.

"Wow," she said, handing the scissors back to the guy.

"Let's load these folks into the ambulance."

"Me too?" Alex asked.

"Please let her come," Mom said. "I couldn't have done this without her. Plus my husband's not home. And I don't want to leave her here alone."

"Okay," the guy with the scissors said. "Come on."

Alex bounded down the stairs ahead of everyone else. It was still dark outside. Alex opened the front door and held it for the paramedics. As she stood there shivering in the darkness, it hit her. *She just delivered a real live baby all by herself.* It was the most important thing she'd ever done in her whole life.

* * *

Three hours later, the sun was just coming up. Alex was trying to fall asleep on a cot in her mother's hospital room, but no matter how hard she tried, she just couldn't sleep. Her brain just kept replaying the incident in the bathroom.

Finally she sat up. Her mother's chest was rising and falling evenly. Mom was asleep.

Alex glanced over at her baby brother's bassinet. She was surprised to discover he was awake.

"You can't sleep either, huh, little guy?" she whispered, resting her chin on the edge of the bassinet.

The baby stared at her intently as though he was trying to figure out where he knew her from.

"I'm Alexandra Alycia Hopewell," she said softly. "Your big sister. I'm the one who caught you when you came out. And I'm the one who moved the umbilical cord away from your neck. But you don't have to thank me. That's what big sisters are for."

The baby blinked. He had a ton of dark hair on his head and really chubby cheeks that reminded Alex of the bottom of an apple. But he was beautiful. So beautiful. And he was *hers*. Her very own baby brother.

Alex leaned over and stroked her finger against his cheek. He turned toward her finger and opened his mouth. Alex let him suck on her pinkie. It tickled. But Alex didn't laugh out loud. She didn't want to wake her mom.

The baby's eyes closed and he fell asleep with Alex's finger still in his mouth. Alex slowly pulled it out.

Such a tiny mouth, she thought. Such a tiny nose and tiny ears and tiny fingers. He was absolutely perfect. The nurse even said so when she weighed and measured him a couple hours earlier.

"Eight pounds, one ounce," she said. "And twenty inches long. I'd say it's a good thing he came a couple weeks early."

"My dad's going to be really surprised," Alex told the nurse. "He's in Germany."

Mom had called the airline as soon as she got to the hospital. They said they'd get Dad on a return flight as soon as they could.

Then the hospital people checked both Mom and the baby. And Mom said they should try and get some sleep. But who could sleep after the night they'd just had?

* * *

"Didn't I tell you not to have that baby while I was gone?" said a voice at the door.

"Dad!" Alex cried. She couldn't see her father behind the five thousand flowers he was carrying, but she knew his voice. She ran to him and threw her arms around his middle.

"John," said Mom. She was sitting up in bed, breastfeeding the baby.

Dad divided his armload of flowers in two. "These are for you," he said, handing Alex one of the bouquets.

"Really?" Alex's eyes grew wide. No one had ever given her flowers before.

"And these," he said, stepping towards Mom, "are for you." He bent to kiss her on the cheek.

Alex grinned. "Guess what, Dad!" she cried, skipping across the room. "I helped get the baby out."

"So I hear," Dad replied. He sat down beside Mom and rested his hand on the baby's head. "Tell me what happened."

"Let me tell it!" Alex cried as she ran to the bed and plopped down between her parents.

She started at the beginning and didn't stop until she got to the end.

Dear Mrs. Ryder,

I'm sorry I broke so many eggs. I didn't mean to. I will pay for them if you want. I know my report on ultrasound wasn't very good. I think this one is better. And I didn't copy any of it out of any book.

Your Student,
Alexandra Alycia Hopewell

Dori Hillestad Butler

Alex Hopewell's Extra Report

Last night my mom had a baby. I was there. I was the only one who was there. Except for my mom. She was there, too.

It happened in the middle of the night. My mom woke me up by screaming AAAAAALEX really loud. I went to find her. She was on the bathroom floor.

She had her nightgown way up around her stomach. She said, "The baby is coming."

I looked. She was right. I saw the baby's hair starting to come out of her.

I called 911. The lady at 911 told me what to do. Everything was okay until I saw the baby's head came out. The umbilical cord was wrapped around the baby's neck. I didn't put it there. The baby just came out like that. I had to get the umbilical cord off or the baby would die. It was hard, but I did it.

I helped my mom and I helped the baby. I'm not as hopeless as everyone thinks. If I can deliver a baby, I can do anything!

P.S. The baby's name is Jacob.

ALEXANDRA HOPEWELL, LABOR COACH

Dear Alexandra,

What a night you and your mother must have had. It sounds like you did everything just right. And this is an excellent report.

Sincerely,
Mrs. Ryder